Gifted To His Dad

A Christmas Novella

J Wilder

The Wilder Ones

Join J. Wilder's Readers' Group Join the Wild Ones readers' group if you love giveaways, polls, teasers, quotes, early access to covers, blurbs and all kinds of other things.

Wilder Ones - J Wilder Reader Group

Author's Note

Hello, wonderful readers!

This book came to be by my desire to just write something fun that doesn't take itself too seriously.

I wanted it to be spicy and sweet.

Something you could devour quickly and finish satisfied. ;)

Have fun.

Happy Smutmas,

xoxo

J.

Dedication

To my readers who want a dash of fun, a sprinkle of
forbidden, and a heaping spoonful of smut.

Chapter 1

Eve

"Wake up, babe. We're here." Cole leans over, guiding a strand of my hair behind my ear. Sleep still holds on to me, and the cab of his truck feels like a warm cocoon I don't want to break out of.

A yawn takes over my face as I come to my senses. "Sorry."

His clear green eyes focus on me as his soft chuckle fills the space. "You're adorable like this."

I don't know how to respond. I've never considered myself anything but ordinary. Boring brown eyes, mid-size frame, with a below-average height. The only thing distinct about me is my copper hair, which my mom swears I inherited from my father. Not that I can remember him. My mom never missed an opportunity to remind me that I was the reason he left her. Apparently, I was colicky as a baby, cried for hours at a time, and he just couldn't take it. Even as an infant, I was too much trouble.

So how am I dating Cole? He's perfect in every way. Captain of our college hockey team. The highest-scoring forward in the division and somehow manages to be at the top of our class in grades. That's not even touching on his popularity. There's not a single person who doesn't know him, or at least wants to know him, on campus. He could have anyone he wants.

So why is he here with me?

"What are you thinking about so seriously?"

I gaze out the windshield at where a mansion of a log cabin stands tall in front of us. Lantern-shaped lights illuminate the rustic details even in the night.

"I don't belong here." I bite my lip, looking anywhere but at him, but he catches my jaw and brings my gaze back to his.

"Don't say that. I've spent weeks begging you to come here. That should be enough to convince you I want you here." He leans over and kisses me gently. His broad frame eclipses mine as his tongue runs along my bottom lip, coaxing my mouth open. The sweet taste of peppermint gum takes over my taste buds as he deepens the kiss. My fingers dig into his shirt, tightening the fabric in my fist as a soft moan escapes my lips.

Tension eases from my shoulders with each stroke

of his tongue. This is the one thing I'm sure of. He wants me. With every touch, he devours me more until I feel like he'll consume me whole, wiping away all my worries.

It's not until my lungs burn for air that he lets me go, resting his forehead against mine. "Let's go in before I fuck you in the car."

I can't stop my smirk. "Wouldn't be the first time."

Before I can pull him back into me, he opens his door, and the crisp winter air sends a chill through me. He somehow convinced me to come to his family's mountain retreat for Christmas break after hearing I wasn't going home to Florida. Cole comes around my side of the car, opening the door and wrapping his arms around me the second I get out. "So...what do you think?"

The full moon casts a glow over the entire area, giving it an almost ethereal look as giant, fluffy snowflakes float down from the sky. I inhale deeply, the cold air stinging my cheeks, but I don't want to break the moment. "It's beautiful."

Cole's gaze is on me, a small smile curving his lips when he responds. "Yeah, you are."

A shiver rolls through me, and Cole entwines our fingers as he leads me up the front steps. He doesn't let go as he punches in the lock code, and the heavy wood door swings inward, revealing a large entryway that's lit by a giant chandelier. Every light is on in the house like someone's here.

I tense, feet sticking to the floor. "I thought you said your stepdad wasn't coming until tomorrow?"

I've been counting on the fact that I'd have an entire day to prepare myself to meet his stepfather. If he's anything like his stepson, I can only imagine how overwhelming it will be. Guys like Cole don't bring girls like me home. We're from different worlds. Not that Cole would ever say that.

He nudges me deeper into the house and shuts the door behind us. "He's not."

I turn my chin up so I can look at him. His six-foot-three height makes it impossible for me to see him eye to eye. He curls his shoulder, cutting the space between us. "I turned the lights on with an app when we got here. I thought you'd be more comfortable that way."

He's sweeter than should be possible, and a tinge of guilt tightens in my chest. It's not fair to him that doubt still creeps in, that somehow none of this feels real. Especially since he's done nothing but be good to me for the last several months.

My fingers tighten in his as we move through the hall to where it opens to an enormous living room. The exposed wood beams at least twenty feet above us look like they're holding the ceiling up. Windows shaped in an A-frame take up the back wall. They're black in the night, but I have no doubt the view is phenomenal.

The focal point of the room is a giant stone fireplace, running floor to ceiling. Large, soft leather sofas flank it, with two extra-deep club chairs in the middle.

"Your mouth's hanging open," Cole says playfully, bumping his shoulder against mine.

My cheeks heat. I've never seen anything like this. "I'm a little overwhelmed."

"Don't worry. You'll get used to it in no time. Think of it as a hotel."

He's trying to soothe me but has no idea I've never been in a hotel that holds a candle to his *vacation* home. I've been to his apartment several times, and even though the furniture is obviously expensive, it didn't make me feel as out of place as I feel here.

Cole's warm arms wrap around me, tugging me against his solid chest. His heart pounds against my ear as he strokes his fingers through my hair.

"Should I not have brought you here? Do you want to go back?"

By his tone, I know he means it. With a word from me, we'll be back on the highway and headed straight home. He's proven time and time again that he'll always take my comfort into account, patiently waiting for me to catch up.

I nuzzle into him, breathing in his deep sandalwood scent, then meet his gaze, giving him my most reassuring smile. "No, I don't want to go. I think I'm just a little tired."

His eyes search mine before he nods. "Okay, let's get you comfortable while I get our things from the truck."

He gestures for me to sit on the sofa, and I climb on, tucked into the corner with my feet pulled under me.

"The doors are going to be open for a bit, so it might get chilly." Cole grabs a blanket from the back of the couch and drapes it over me, then leans down to light a log in the fireplace before walking out toward the car.

It's surreal being here, in a place I would never have imagined being invited, with a guy I'd never imagined would be interested in me. I cut off those thoughts and pull the blanket higher as I rest against the armrest. I promised I wouldn't be so hard on myself. That I would finally accept the good things that have been happening in my life. I moved across the country to get away from the past, and I will not let it hold me back.

Cole comes back, his warm breath fanning over my forehead before soft lips press against my skin.

"Are you nervous?" he hums against my neck, his nose running up the column until he grazes my ear. "I can help you with that."

Tingles follow the path, raising goose bumps in their wake.

His startling green eyes are as deep as the forest in the warm light. "I can't tell you how delicious you look wrapped up on my couch. Like a gift just waiting to be unwrapped."

Warmth fills my veins at his words, and I open the blanket and spread my knees in invitation.

He groans deep in the back of his throat and climbs between them, his weight pressing me down into the cushions. His thumb runs along my bottom lip, and I suck it into my mouth, causing his hips to grind into me.

"You're already hard." My voice is a whisper as he rocks his hips.

"Of fucking course I am. I finally have you all to myself." He leans in and kisses me until I surrender to him. His warmth takes over, chasing away any remaining chill.

"You're beautiful," he hums, then takes my breath again, filling my mouth. Our movements grow frantic with each time his cock rubs against my clit. I cling to him, his shirt balled up in my fist, but it's not enough. I need to hold him, feel his skin against mine. I tug at the shirt until he sits up, wearing a cocky smile.

It's well-earned. My heart nearly stops as the fabric clears his chest, revealing row upon row of defined muscles. No matter how many times I see him, I can never get used to it. His tanned skin glows in the soft light, and it feels unfair that he's so freaking hot.

I wrap my hands around my middle, stopping him from lifting my shirt.

"I think we should leave it on."

He raises one dark brow, then leans forward, kissing my hands, before peeling them away one at a time. I swallow hard as his hand travels under my shirt, tracing the roundness of my stomach, then moves upward. He cups my breast and squeezes, drawing out my gasp.

"Don't you dare hide your body from me."

Within seconds, my shirt's over my head, leaving me exposed, but instead of feeling self-conscious, his dark gaze warms me to the core. He bites the corner of his lip as he takes me in. "You're perfect."

My skin flushes with his words. I know I'm anything but perfect, but that doesn't stop the ache in my lower stomach.

I arch my head, falling back, giving in. "Touch me."

"Fuck yes," he growls, mouth descending on my lace-covered nipples. I'd worn this bra for him, but nothing could prepare me for the way his hot tongue soaking the fabric would make me feel.

With each stroke of his tongue, I press my hips up, no longer able to control their movements. A tiny voice in the back of my head reminds me we're in the living room and we should not be doing this, but I have no will to listen.

His hand slides under my waistband and panties, moving directly to my core. Thick fingers slide through my folds, spreading my wetness until I'm soaked with it. I barely have a second to breathe before he's pushing two thick fingers into me, stealing my breath.

"Cole," I gasp, only driving him further.

His fingers stroke deeper, filling me completely. "That's it. Say my name. Tell me what you need."

"More," I plead, and he gives it to me, adding another finger, stretching me wide.

The burn quickly turns into pleasure, and my hips rock against him, urging him faster.

"Come on my hand," he demands as he grinds his palm into my clit.

Tension explodes from my core up my spine, sending tingles throughout my limbs. My voice cracks as I cry out his name with my release over and over.

He's sliding my leggings down my thighs while I greedily undo his pants.

I jolt when someone clears their throat behind us.

"I thought I would surprise you, but it looks like I'm the one getting a surprise." His voice is a deeper timber, the sound seeping into my bones. There's maturity in it that unfortunately gives away who the man is, even without looking. I bury my face in Cole's chest, and he bands an arm around me.

"Eve, this is my stepdad, Griffin."

Chapter 2

Cole

"IT'S NOT THAT BAD." I wrap my arms around Eve where she's cocooned in the blankets. Her entire body, including her head, is covered, and she's pulled her knees up into a tight ball. I try to lower the covers to see her face, but she holds on to it tight. "Come out, babe. I promise you it's fine."

"I'm never coming out," she groans, mortification clear in her voice, and makes herself even smaller.

Wishing she'd allow me under the covers with her, I squeeze her knee tight. I hate she feels this way. "I promise Griffin doesn't care."

"We were on his *couch*! He saw everything... He saw me..." Her voice drops to barely a whisper. "Orgasm."

I kiss her forehead, wishing I could do anything to

13

fix this, but I can't turn back time. "Babe, don't be embarrassed. I can't stand it."

"Embarrassed doesn't even begin to encapsulate what I'm feeling right now. I think I'll just stay here until I die. You'll have to bring me food and water."

A low chuckle forms in the back of my throat. She's so adorable sometimes. I can't help but love her. Not that she's ready to hear that yet. My girl is skittish, and I'm sure this isn't helping. "You have to come out, eventually."

"Never." The blankets move in what I assume is her shaking her head no.

I lift off her and sit on the side of the bed. It's clear nothing but time will coax her out. I slide my hands under her, tucking the blankets in. "How about this? I'll go talk to him and make sure everything is all good, and you can hide in here for now."

"Okay, but if it's weird, we're leaving." Her voice trembles, like she's asking too much.

I hate that she feels that way. I'm not sure how I'm going to do it, but I swear I'll prove to her she can ask me anything. No...that she *deserves* everything. I kiss her head through the cover. "I promise. If it's too uncomfortable, just let me know, and we'll leave first thing."

I leave the room, shutting the door quietly behind

me, and run my hand through my hair. This was *not* the way I expected to start this weekend.

I go through the hall that separates the bedroom from the main area to find a smiling Griffin waiting for me in the kitchen.

My brows pull down, and I cross my arms over my chest. "You weren't supposed to be here until tomorrow."

Griffin looks behind me to where the hallway leads to the guest room. "I didn't mean to embarrass her."

"She'll be fine. She's cool like that. Just needs a bit of time. Be nice to her."

His eyes are still fixed behind me, but now there's a darkened look to them. "That won't be a problem."

Testing the waters, I ask, "She's hot, right?"

Griffin and I didn't meet until I was already nineteen, so there's always been something special about how we interact. Somehow, we're closer than most people I know. My mom abandoned us both, and Griffin's the one who stepped in when I needed a place to stay. I'm looking for something more than his approval. I want him to see her the way I do. No matter how fucked-up that is.

A muscle ticks in Griffin's jaw. "I think it's better I don't answer that."

I hum in the back of my throat, pushing him just a

little further. "She's sweet too. Wait until you get to know her."

It's fucked-up, but I need him to like her. More than I should. I search him for signs of being uncomfortable, anything that shows he doesn't like the way the conversation is going, but he just looks past me again.

His gaze goes hooded, and then he clears his throat. "Let's get dinner started, then you can go get her."

I join him in the kitchen, our movements coordinated after years of living together. I duck naturally as he reaches over me, his back grazing my shirt. A shiver runs down my spine at his closeness. I'm not attracted to him, but there's something about him being near that's always interested me. Like I want to share more with him than is normal.

He pulls back, holding a large salad bowl in his hand, and cool air replaces his heat. He puts it on the table and gestures to me. "Handle this, and I'll take care of the steaks."

I give him a quick nod and get to work on cutting the vegetables, making a spring salad to go with the meat and potatoes. I glance at the clock for the fifth time. I can't stand being away from Eve even for a second, and at this point, I don't care who knows it. By the way she stays close to me, I'm sure she feels the same.

I finish mixing in the dressing when Griffin bumps his shoulder against mine. "Go get your girl so we can get the awkwardness over with."

I'm not exactly sure how this will work, but I put down the tongs and make my way back to our room.

Eve's still wrapped up in a ball when I enter, and I climb over her, unwrapping her like a present. Her cheeks are still flushed when she looks up at me.

I brush a strand of her hair back. "I talked to Griffin. I told you it would be fine."

"Really?" She bites the corner of her lip, and it takes all my willpower to stop from running my thumb along it, freeing it from her teeth.

"Really. He knows he should have texted us first. He feels guilty that he embarrassed you like that. So come out and help put him out of his misery."

It's wrong of me to play on her people-pleasing tendencies, but she'd stay in here forever, given the opportunity.

"Promise to stay with me? Don't leave my side."

"I'd never dream of leaving."

I get up, and I'm so proud of my girl when she kicks off her blankets. I know how hard this is for her. How shy she can be. Even at school, she seems to hide behind me, almost acting like she's not there. It's more than just shyness. It's like she doesn't believe she belongs by my side, and I will do everything in my power to prove just how wrong she is. If the people around us can't see how perfect she is, that's on them.

Taking her hand, I lead her through the hall and give her a little tug when she pauses.

She follows me, tucking herself close, and I wrap my arm around her, enjoying the way her body molds to mine.

Griffin looks up from the grill and gives her a warm smile. "Hi, I'm Griffin. It's nice to finally meet you. Cole hasn't stopped talking about you."

Her gaze meets mine, a soft flush taking over her cheeks, and I lean down to whisper in her ear.

"I told you I'm head over heels for you."

Chapter 3

Eve

Goose bumps rise along my neck as Cole's breath fans over my sensitive skin. He's a little too close for being in front of his stepdad, but I can't help but relax at his words. He's been doing everything he can to make me feel comfortable since we met. I cling to him when I finally face Griffin, still unable to meet his gaze.

"Nice to meet you. I'm Eve." I'm proud that I stopped my voice from cracking. No need to make this any more embarrassing than it already is. I'm about to apologize when Griffin cuts in.

"I'm sorry. I should have let Cole know I was coming in early today. I didn't mean to give you such a shock." He says it in a low timber that sends a shiver down my spine.

My body tenses at its reaction, and it's only Cole's

thumb grazing back and forth on the back of my neck that stops me from running back to the room.

"I told you it wasn't a big deal." Cole kisses the top of my head, our height difference standing out with the action. He's at least half a foot taller than me, and by the looks of it, Griffin is even taller. I finally get the courage to look at him, and my breath catches in my throat. The same way it did when I first saw Cole.

He's broad, his shoulders spanning several feet across, the muscles underneath stretching his navy henley shirt. His sleeves are rolled up, revealing thick forearms with defined veins that have me wanting to touch them. Heat warms my chest as my gaze travels upward over the thick tendons of his neck to his brown hair, slightly graying at the temples. Cole mentioned he was in his late forties, but somehow, that just makes him hotter. *Shit.* I definitely shouldn't be thinking about him like this. I am a horrible girlfriend. The *worst.*

Cole's hand wraps around the back of my neck, giving it a small squeeze, easing some of my discomfort. There's no way he hasn't noticed me check out his stepdad, but for whatever reason, he doesn't seem to mind.

Griffin's crisp blue eyes glimmer as he smiles at me, catching me checking him out.

Heat crawls up my neck and into my cheeks. I'm

frozen in place, unable to move from this spot where I feel like a deer caught in headlights. The moment snaps when my stomach growls loudly, giving away the fact that I haven't eaten all day.

Cole pulls me into his chest before saying, "Now that introductions are over, let's eat."

They don't let me help as they set up the table, spreading out the food. Cole takes his time filling my plate for me, careful to choose the best steak.

It's a pale pink in the center, a perfect medium, just how I like it. Baked, seasoned baby potatoes right out of the oven and a fresh salad on the side. My mouth's already watering as I take my first bite. A soft hum forms at the back of my throat.

Both men look at me, their gazes focused on my mouth. I swallow hard, ignoring the warmth traveling down my stomach.

I already knew Cole doesn't speak to his mom and is much closer to Griffin, but I've always wanted to know more. I clear my throat. "So, how did you two meet? Cole told me a little about it but not the details."

They look at each other as if in a silent conversation before coming back to me.

Griffin is the first to respond. "I made the mistake of marrying Cole's mother after only knowing her for a few months. I didn't even have time to meet Cole at that point since he'd been out of the country. It wasn't until he was nineteen and moved back home that I really got to know him. Unfortunately, that lined up with his mother taking off and sending me divorce papers a week later."

I expect him to look sad about it. After all, having a whirlwind relationship that ended up in a quick marriage sounds like the stuff from romance novels, but he looks bored with it. Like it's just a random part of his past.

Unsure what to say, I default to, "I'm sorry that happened."

Griffin grunts, noncommittal. "It's fine."

"Plus, you got me out of the deal." Cole grins, not a worry in the world, not a doubt that Griffin is happy to have him in his life.

I know exactly how much it can hurt to have a parent abandon you, but if it affected Cole, he doesn't show it.

The big man across from me wears a hint of a smirk. "There's that."

"You two seem close." I dig a little deeper, unable to stop my eternal curiosity, no matter how much I try. I just hope I'm not prying too much.

"Definitely. Even without really knowing me, Griffin took me in and let me stay with him for the year before I headed off to college. I really don't know what I would have done if he hadn't. It's not like I could get a hold of my mom, and I never met my biological father. My mother always gave a different description of who he was. So I was basically screwed. Well, I would have been if Griffin didn't take me in, feed, clothe me, and pay for my schooling."

I take the glass of wine Griffin passes to me, his large hand engulfing the glass. His fingers graze mine, sending unwanted tingles down my arm. I should not be reacting to him, not when Cole's sitting right beside me.

I clear my throat, trying to pull myself together. "So that was four years ago? You must really feel like family now."

Both men take large gulps of their beers, Cole answering first. "You could say we've bonded over the years."

I tilt my head, trying to read the look that passes between them. There's something left unsaid, like they're speaking their own language. I can't begin to figure it out.

Griffin clears his throat, asking, "How about you? Your folks live by the college?"

My gut twists, driving acid up my throat. I hate talking about my family. Nothing good ever comes from it. For some reason, I really don't want this man to know my father abandoned me. That he found me unworthy of being loved.

Cole squeezes my thigh under the table, then pulls me close so he can whisper, "You know you don't have to worry about us. Griffin won't judge you for your asshole father. If anything, he'd track him down and beat his ass."

"Track who down?" Griffin's deep timber is edged as he leans closer, startling me.

I didn't realize he could overhear us. The wine tastes bitter as I finish off my glass, and Cole fills it again.

"My dad took off when I was younger, and my mom was never really around. She had several jobs, and I'm grateful that she could support me." I leave out the fact that she made it known every day that I was the reason she had to work so much. If it wasn't for me, my father never would have left her.

I don't notice I've finished another glass of wine until Griffin takes it. "Something tells me that's not the whole story."

I shrug, not sure how to respond to that without cutting myself open and showing all the damaged parts of me. There's something about these two men that makes me feel like it wouldn't be such a bad thing, like they'd help put me back together if I just trusted them.

"You look a little flushed. Maybe we should call it a night." Cole's warm thumb grazes over my cheek, and I lean into his touch.

26

It's not lost on me how hard he's working to show me I can trust him. That he wants me here just as much as I want to be here.

I go to stand but wobble on my feet, blood rushing to my head. A strong, solid arm bands around my back, catching me and surrounding me in the fresh scent of forest.

Cole's standing in front of me, a sly smirk forming on his lips. It takes my sluggish brain several seconds to realize what's happened, and my head snaps up, meeting Griffin's piercing blue eyes. There's an electric tension surrounding us and holding me in place as heat pools between my thighs. He's staring down at me, bottom lip caught between his teeth, a muscle ticking in his jaw as if he's fighting something, before he finally lets me go, pushing me toward Cole.

His voice is gruff when he says, "Get some sleep," then turns on his heels and disappears down the hall.

The loss of his warmth is like an ice bath snapping me back to reality. What did I just do? I stare at the ground, unable to meet Cole's gaze. He's going to hate me for this. There's no way he didn't notice how I was reacting to Griffin's touch. I suck in a breath, trying to ready myself for what comes next.

Cole's gentle touch guides my chin up. His lips skim mine, drawing my attention to him.

"You are so freaking hot right now," he says huskily

as he slides his hand under my shirt and strokes the bare skin at my waist.

Startled, I go to pull away, but he holds me in place, eyes darkened on me as his hand slowly ascends my rib cage.

His voice is dark, liquid as he says, "The way pink curls up your neck and your breath comes out in shallow pants is driving me crazy."

He captures my mouth in a demanding kiss, pushing his tongue deep, claiming me. All thoughts are lost to his touch, as if he's controlling me down to the beating of my heart.

Hands grip my ass, pulling me up until my legs wrap around his hips. I gasp in a breath as his hard cock grinds into me, the pressure directly against my clit. His movements turn wild as he touches me everywhere, leaving hot trails of desire in their wake. I've never been so grateful to have a birth control implant.

The faint sound of a shower turning on has me pulling away. "We should go to the room."

He drops his head to mine, taking several breaths before releasing his grip and letting my feet settle on the ground. "You've got two seconds to run before I strip you right here."

I swallow hard and rush down the hall, knowing he's only a step behind me. We're no more than a foot into the room before the door slams and he has me pushed up against it, mouth instantly hot on mine. We only break apart to rip off my shirt and bra before pushing my leggings and thong to the ground.

He pulls back to look at me, growling deep in his throat. "So fucking pretty."

His mouth encircles my nipple as he sucks on it hard, drawing a tight scream from me. It hurts, but I don't want him to stop. My fingers tangle in his pants, desperately trying to push them down. He chuckles and pushes them the rest of the way until his cock rests against my core.

His face is so close that his breaths mingle with mine as he coats his cock with my wetness. "Fuck, baby."

He pushes my thighs tight together, trapping his cock between them, his eyes dark as he slides it back and forth.

With each push of his hips, the base of his cock rubs against my clit, drawing pleasure through my body until it forms a tight knot within me.

Cole's breaths grow sharp, his movements jerky as he pounds me into the door. Clear green eyes consume me as he pulls us closer to our release. I've never done anything like this. I didn't know something that's almost innocent could feel this amazing. My fingers dig into his shoulders, the thin fabric doing nothing to stop my nails from bruising him.

I moan and cover my mouth, trying to stop the sounds from escaping.

He pulls it away, nipping my bottom lip. "I want to hear you."

My next moan is even louder, but at this point, I don't care. My hips move on their own, practically begging him for more.

"Come for me," he demands, and like he controls me, my body responds with electricity shooting through me until I see stars.

He pulls back, covering my stomach with his own release. His head drops to mine as he massages his cum into my skin with his fingers.

"You look good like this."

I can barely hold myself up, and he supports me with an arm around my back. I heave in breaths, trying to regain a semblance of rationality.

"We should shower." My voice is barely above a whisper.

He shakes his head no. "I'm not even close to being done with you."

I look down, shocked that he's still so hard.

"Don't look so surprised." He lifts me easily, dropping me on the bed, then pulls off his shirt.

My mouth waters. No matter how many times I see him, I can never get used to how hot he is. He's covered in muscles that fit his broad frame perfectly.

He lifts my hand and drags it down his stomach, giving me a cocky smile. "Like what you see?"

I roll my eyes. "You already know the answer to that."

He reaches down and pinches my nipple. "Doesn't mean I don't like to hear it."

"Yes."

"Yes, what?" he asks as he lifts me by my thighs so my ass is off the bed and my legs are pressed together, draped over his one shoulder where he stands.

I narrow my eyes, answering him. "Yes, you're hot."

"That's my girl." He drives his cock into me all the way to the base.

My lungs cave in with the force, and my head grows weak as I struggle to take in a breath. He's too big, too deep, too much, at the same time somehow not enough.

"Move," I plead, and he instantly pulls out before pushing back into me.

I expect him to be fast, but it's almost painfully slow, driving me crazy with each thrust.

"*Please.*"

I'm lifted to the center of the bed and flipped over onto my hands and knees before he enters me, filling me completely. He's even deeper at this angle, and it's almost too much to take.

"You have no idea what you do to me when you

beg like that." He grips my hips and slams himself into me, sending blood rushing to my head until my vision darkens on the verge of passing out.

I don't want him to stop. I've never been this turned on in my life.

He wraps his arm around my breast and pulls my back to his chest. The new angle is even more intense. He pushes two fingers between my teeth, burying them in my mouth. I suck the taste off them, moaning as they take over the same way his cock drives into my pussy.

The sensation is overwhelming, and my mind begins to black out, the view in front of me replaced with something else.

Something I shouldn't be thinking of. Something off-limits.

My imagination turns Cole's fingers into Griffin's thick cock, pushing deep into my throat. He's wide and hot as he fills my mouth. I run my tongue over the underside, swirling it, and he pushes deeper until I gag and my eyes water. He doesn't pull back, repeating the motion again and again.

I moan, my hips rocking back into Cole's cock while his stepdad takes my mouth.

Cole's thick fingers graze my clit before flanking where his cock is entering me. "Your pussy is clenching around me, and you're dripping down my sides. What kind of naughty thoughts are you having?"

Guilt pulls me back to reality, but Cole doesn't remove his fingers, instead adding a third, stretching my mouth almost painfully.

"Do you want someone to fuck your mouth while I pound your pussy?"

I cry out as my orgasm slams into me, over and over again with a force I've never experienced.

Hot liquid fills me as Cole follows me over the edge.

My head collapses back, my limbs unable to move as shivers still make their way down my spine.

Cole's teeth nip my ear. "Never hold anything back from me again. I want every dirty part of you. It's all mine."

His words fill me with warmth, a seductive sense of security that I want to hold on to. I nod in agreement, unable to utter a word. I'm beyond exhausted. I've chased the approval of men for most of my life, but nothing compares to him.

He wraps me in his arms, pulling my face to his chest and draping the blankets over us. My fingers trail the marks I left on him, and I'm filled with the need to leave more. To mark him for anyone to see. I've never wanted to belong to anyone, but if it's him, I think I'd be okay with it. I think I'd feel safe.

Chapter 4

Griffin

THE PIECE of wood slices in two as the impact from the ax reverberates up my arms. I toss the pieces into the ever-growing pile on my right. I've been out here since sunrise, unable to sleep. Every time I close my eyes, I see her perfect fucking body, soft hips, curved waist, and luscious fucking tits. She gives me that sweet, shy smile, and I'm done for. I'll never get the sound of her out of my head as Cole made her scream over and over again. I should never have picked the room beside theirs, but I couldn't bring myself to change it. Not when my cock was rock hard in my hand, listening to them. Sleep became impossible, even after they stopped.

I swing my arms down in an arc, and the wood easily splinters under the sharpened blade of the ax.

I came out here this morning to try to clear my

head, some physical labor to work away my thoughts. Sweat forms on my brow. It feels like I'm burning from the inside out, and I pull off my shirt, the cold a distant worry, and wipe my face with it.

Footsteps come up beside me, and Cole stands a piece of wood on the stump beside me.

"Morning." Even though he's not looking at me, he's wearing a mischievous smirk, and his voice is teasing.

Another piece of wood splinters beneath my ax, and I reply with a grunt. "Morning."

This kid's the reason I haven't slept, and he knows it. "I could hear you last night."

He chuckles as he sets up another log. "I know. I made her scream just for you."

"It fucking worked. I haven't jerked off like that since I was your age." I groan, adjusting my jeans. "I'm fucking still hard." I can't escape the images of how her sweet little mouth would have looked making those sounds for him. How she'd feel pressed between us, taking us at the same time. Would her nails dig into my back as she screamed our names? The thought is entirely too addictive. Once I start, I'm not sure I can stop.

I chop another piece, my muscles burning as I ask, "You think she's the one?"

"I do. I love her."

Two years ago, Cole walked in on me fucking someone and freaked the fuck out. I couldn't make sense of it at first. Sure, it was awkward, but we were both adults by then. It wasn't until she was gone and he came home piss drunk that I understood. He didn't want any girl to come between us. At first, I didn't understand. It's not like we were going to be celibate, and no matter how much he's grown, I'm not interested in fucking my own son. When I'd pulled back and told him it was never going to happen, he gripped my arms, yelling at me to listen. He didn't want us to be a couple. He wanted to find a girl to share *between* us. To become a part of our family. Integrated just as much as we are. Someone who fits perfectly, like a puzzle piece that solidifies our life forever. A sick, twisted, perverted part of me liked that idea entirely too much. Someone we could both cherish, who could fill that deep void that exists in both of us. If he says Eve can be that girl, I can't deny I want it, but not at the expense of Cole's happiness.

He turns to me, raising a brow. "Don't lie to me and tell me you're not interested."

When did he start reading me so easily? "I am."

"Alright, let's move forward."

There's a spark in his eyes, an excitement I haven't seen in a long time. He really cares for this girl. I can see why. It's only been a day, and I can already feel myself falling under her spell.

"You said you love her? This can easily blow up in our faces. We're asking a lot from her. Are you willing to risk losing her? Are you really prepared to lose someone you love?"

He drops his ax to the ground and rubs his hands over his face, then through his hair. He looks miserable when he responds. "If she leaves, then she wasn't the right one to begin with."

"You know I'll be okay if you choose her. You don't have to do this just because we agreed. It's not some kind of blood pact."

"Fuck off. I saw the way she was looking at you. I'm pretty sure she was picturing you last night by the way she sucked on my fingers like you were fucking her mouth."

I groan, my cock painfully hard. If he keeps saying shit like that, I won't be able to control myself. We don't want to scare her away. "We can't approach this head-on. She needs to have time to get used to it."

"It's about time you came around. This is the only type of family I want, and I know she'll be game. I'm telling you she's meant for us. She just needs to get to know you a bit."

"Get back to work." I cut wood until my arms burn

and sweat rolls down my back. The more I think about it, the more I think Cole's right. She's the one for us.

Chapter 5

Eve

THE DEEP AROMA of coffee fills my nose as I step out of my room. I rolled over only to find Cole wasn't there. Instead, he'd tucked the blankets around me. A quick glance at the clock tells me I slept in way later than usual.

Making my way into the kitchen, I pour myself a coffee, eyes still half-closed when I glance out the window, my mouth instantly dropping open.

Cole and Griffin are out there chopping wood... *shirtless*. Snow is all around them, but sweat still runs down their flexing muscles. They move in unison as they chop through each piece, filling the enormous pile beside them. From the look of it, they've been out there for hours. My mouth waters so much I'm surprised I'm not drooling. I can't take my eyes off either man. I should feel guilty looking at Griffin when Cole's right there, but there's something about the two of them being so close together that has heat pooling between my thighs. My knees nearly give out when they toss their axes and Griffin pulls Cole into a side hug. I spin around before I do something stupid and hold myself up with a hand against the counter. I don't think I could live through seeing that again.

The back door opens, Cole coming in first, making his way right to me. "Morning, Eve." He hugs me tight, and his sweat gets all over me.

"Gross." I push back, even though there's nothing about his musky scent that has me wanting to pull away. The problem is if I keep touching him, I won't be able to stop.

Cole kisses my forehead, then lets me go and takes the bottle of water Griffin holds out for him, draining it in a few big gulps.

"I'm going to shower. We have somewhere special to bring you today."

Curiosity pulls at me. "Can't you tell me now?"

"Nope. It's a surprise." He chuckles low in his throat. "Get your stuff. We won't be long."

I take my time finishing my coffee while looking for my things. Unable to clear my mind of Cole and Griffin shirtless and chopping wood, I walk on autopilot to the bedroom. I thought I had my mittens in my purse, but I must have packed them in my luggage. I open the door, planning on sneaking in and out, but I freeze.

Griffin's standing in the middle of the room with nothing on besides a white towel covering his face as he dries his hair. Alarm bells ring in my head, telling me to run, but I can't pull myself away. Thick muscles ripple as his arms move, his abs flexing where they turn in a V leading to his massive cock. He's thick and long, with defined veins running up his length. My heart's racing in my chest, a heavy lust rushing through my stomach, heading straight to my core. It practically begs me to touch it, to apply the friction my clit desperately needs. I squeeze my legs together as the desire grows more intense.

"I think you're in the wrong room, Baby Girl." He's staring at me with dark eyes, not looking away.

Reality slams into me. Holy shit.

"I'm sorry," I squeak and rush out of the room, barely escaping what could have easily become my undoing.

I shut the bedroom door behind me, leaning against the wall as I struggle to catch my breath. My clit's still pulsing with the need to be touched.

Cole steps out of the bathroom, towel wrapped

around his waist. He approaches, stealing the space in front of me until the rivulets of water dampen my shirt. His thumb runs along my cheek before he places a gentle kiss to my lips.

"You okay? You look a little flushed."

The lust I felt a minute ago is replaced with guilt. How could I do this to him? He's been so perfect this entire time, and I'm being an idiot.

"I'm sorry," I whisper.

He slides his thumb along my bottom lip, causing my heart to skip. "There's nothing to be sorry about so long as you're fine."

Why does it sound like he knows exactly what happened? Like he'd be okay with it. It can't be. There's no boyfriend who would be okay with what I just did.

I should tell him.

I should beg him for his forgiveness, but I can't.

I'm too selfish, and I don't want to lose him.

I drop my head to his chest and breathe him in, taking comfort in the way he wraps his arms around me. I just won't do anything like that again.

I lift my head, tilting it back. "I forgot my mittens here."

He gently knocks me under my chin, then rubs my hands between his. "Can't have you missing those."

I give him a weak smile, unable to meet his gaze. There's barely enough room for me to squeeze out around him, and I grab my mittens as quickly as I can before rushing from the room. Why does it feel like I'm always escaping today?

Chapter 6

Eve

COLE HANDS me a travel coffee mug as I climb into the back of Griffin's Range Rover. He explained that they had a surprise for me but won't tell me what. The only thing I know for sure is I had to dress warmly. So, decked out in my winter coat, mittens, and boots, I watch out the window as the SUV winds through twisty mountain roads. It looks different from how it did on the way here, the light reflecting off the snow-capped trees making everything appear like it's been pulled out of a painting.

Within minutes, we're pulling up to a wood building with a green metal roof. The parking lot is full of idling trucks, exhaust steaming from their tailpipes. A family of five jumps out of the vehicle beside us, the kids grinning as their mom helps them with their gloves. Their excitement is almost palpable through the glass.

"Do you know what we're doing yet?" Griffin asks from where he's turned in the driver's seat to look back at me. Cole is beside him, giving me a warm smile.

I'd been too lost in what was happening outside to notice. "Um..." I glance around, looking for clues, and through the rows of cars, I can make out a large sign that's written in red cursive: "Mary's Christmas Trees."

A childish joy builds in my chest as my eyes focus around me. Finally, I notice the men all carry saws in their hands and rope.

"We're getting a tree?" I can't hold back my giddiness. They must think I'm losing it. Grown women shouldn't be this excited about something so common as a Christmas tree, but everything about this experience is new to me.

Griffin's crisp blue eyes search my face, and he softens. "Sure are, Baby Girl. You get to pick."

The nickname does something to my insides, and I glance at Cole to see how he's going to react. I half expected him to be setting up to knock his stepdad out, but he's giving me a loose, happy smile. Like everything is going exactly his way.

I climb out of the back seat, boots crunching on snow as my feet hit the ground. A gust of wind swirls by, lifting the corner of my beanie with it, sending a shiver down my spine.

Griffin's quick to act, catching the knitted fabric before it can escape.

"Wouldn't want to lose this," he says as he slips my hat back in place.

The goose bumps that rise along my neck have nothing to do with the cold and everything to do with how his fingers graze the underside of my jaw as he pulls back.

"We ready? Let's go." Strong arms wrap around me from behind, and Cole drops his chin to the top of my head. His warmth soaks through my coat, and I find myself instantly relaxing into him. He has a way of making everything feel fun, like there's never a reason to hide the fact that you're enjoying yourself.

Completely foreign to the way I was brought up, where image was everything to my mother, presenting a perfect package to whatever man she was interested in. Which included a near silent child who'd sit quietly, never too excited.

Cole's fingers intertwine with mine, and he pulls me after him. "First one in gets to pick the tree."

He lets go and dashes down the aisle between the cars, and I chase after him.

"Hey! Griffin already said I could."

Cole disappears ahead of me, my five-foot-five

stature making it impossible for me to keep up. I'm panting as my run slows to a jog, barely faster than a walk, when Cole wraps his arms around me and swings me in a hug.

"That's not fair," I say breathlessly.

He hums in the back of his throat and smirks. "I'll let you win for a kiss."

His lips are already on mine before I can respond. It starts off soft but quickly builds until my fingers curl into his jacket.

"Save it for at home, you two. This is a family event," Griffin says, his voice light as he grabs my waist, pulling me away from Cole.

Heat curls up my cheeks, no doubt turning them a ruby red as embarrassment takes over. "Sorry."

He squeezes the curve of my hip through the thick fabric of my coat before letting go. "Never apologize for doing what feels good. Now, hurry before all the good ones are gone."

They may have said I could pick, but each time I pointed a tree out, both men told me we could find a bigger, fuller, better one if we just looked a little harder.

My toes are frozen solid by the time we reach the back row.

Cole lets out a long, low whistle. "This. Is. The. One."

It's freaking massive. I have to crane my neck to see the tip of the tree, standing at least twelve feet in the air. The base is as wide as my spread arms.

My mouth drops open. "Are you sure...? Can we even make it fit?"

"Just need to be patient. We can always make it fit." Cole winks at me, and I can feel my face flame.

Griffin clears his throat and looks away, but I can see the way his mouth curls into a grin.

"I guess I walked into that," I grumble.

They do some magic where they tie the tree to a different tree, then cut on a precise angle so it lowers safely in the direction they want. The branches hit the ground with a soft thud, snow lifting around us like a cloud. When my vision clears, the Christmas tree looks even bigger from the ground.

"How are we going to move that?" I ask.

"I'll help you." A boy who can't be older than seventeen comes up and arranges his sled beside the massive tree. It takes all three of them to roll it on.

"You two go get some hot chocolate. I'll help him get it wrapped, and we can meet at the car," Griffin says as he grabs the end of the rope with the kid, and they drag the weight behind them.

"You heard the man. Hot chocolate."

Inside, the building is warm and cozy. The entire place looks like Santa's village. Trees decorated to show off ornaments for purchase. Aisles with everything from cookie cutters to wreaths. There's a glow forming in my chest, and the back of my eyes begin to burn as I watch the families weave through the space.

Cole comes up to me, holding out a Styrofoam cup, steam pouring from the top, and leads me out into the parking lot.

He takes one look at me and raises his hand to my face, wiping under my eye. "What's wrong?"

"Everything is perfect." I know it doesn't make any sense, but I can't explain it any other way.

"So, am I included in all this perfection?" He gives me a cocky smile.

I choke on my laugh, doing my best not to spill my hot chocolate. "I guess so."

He wraps me in his arms and pulls me close, nuzzling my ear. "You guess so, hm? What do I need to do to make you certain?"

My breath catches as his low timber curls in my stomach.

"I can't leave you two alone for a second," Griffin says from beside us, scolding. "Get in the car."

"Yes, Daddy." I say it out of reflex, and my eyes go wide.

It's their hooded eyes, hot on me, that tell me I've done something unexpected. Griffin closes the distance between us until the toes of his boots brush mine, my back pressing into Cole's chest. Time slows around us as Cole gently grips my hips, holding me in place as Griffin leans in closer. Tingling electricity crackles beneath my skin as anticipation swirls below my ribs. I'm not sure what's about to happen, but I know I'm waiting for it. Each second feels like an eternity. If I just stay still, maybe I can have it.

"Excuse me." A young mother comes by us with a stroller, and I jerk away.

I cover my face with my hands. What was I thinking?

The ride home is uneventful. The guys laugh with each other in the front seat. It's easy and oh so natural. It's clear that they've been doing this for years. A twinge forms in my chest as I watch them, wondering what it must be like to have a family you can be close to. If I look deeper, I can admit that I'm not just jealous of what they have; I want to be a part of it with them. For them to accept me in their family for longer than just a weekend. Cole and I will go back to the city. He'll stay in his apartment while I'll be at my rundown one, and that loneliness will sneak back in...

Cole turns in his seat until he can face me. "You're quiet. Everything okay?"

How does he always know when I've gotten too far into my head? How does he always know how to pull me out?

"Just a little tired."

His brow twitches like he doesn't believe me, but his voice is soft when he says, "We'll get you home, and you can read your book while we set up this tree."

"I can help," I protest.

Griffin says, "No way. You aren't going anywhere near that thing until we get it stabilized."

I'd argue, but who am I kidding? I'm more than happy to sit back and read while they figure it out.

We pull into the cabin's long driveway and park in front. The guys are already bickering about the best way to get it down before they get out.

Griffin guides me to where he's deemed a safe distance away. "Stay here."

There's a command in his tone, and I fight back the urge to say *yes, Daddy* again. A small part of me wants to see if their reaction is even more intense. I get the distinct feeling I'm playing with fire, but I don't have time to think too hard about it before the tree's sliding off the hood of the car and the end swings out, coming my way.

Even with the distance, I can tell I can't avoid the hit, and I lift my arms to protect myself. I'm pushed back, flattened against the side of the house, pinned in place by a broad, heaving chest.

Griffin's muscles flex like he's holding himself back before he lets out a long breath. "Fuck, that could have been bad." He lifts my chin and checks me for injuries. "You okay?"

"Y... yes." I barely get out the words, lungs refusing to work while he's still so close.

"Sorry to break it up. You'll have to continue your cute moment later. I need some help over here," Cole says from where he's holding the tree in an attempt to stop it from tilting further.

Griffin glances at my lips one more time before pulling back and shaking his head. "Alright, kiddo. I'm coming."

"Who are you calling kiddo, old man?" Cole grunts out under the heavy weight.

It takes some intricate maneuvering, but they finally manage to get it down and onto their own makeshift sled.

Cole comes up to me, his chest rising and falling rapidly as he tries to catch his breath. "Why don't you go inside and get comfy while we do the rest?"

"Are you sure you don't need any help?" I ask.

He tucks a strand of my hair behind my ear and pulls my beanie lower. "We'll just worry about you if you're out here."

I glance at Griffin, and he nods.

"Okay then. I'll see you inside."

It doesn't take long for my book to ease my mind, helping me settle into the couch. The world is fading into the distance with each chapter I consume. The living room is large, so I'm seated far enough away that I'm not in any danger of being struck by a stray branch. It's only when Cole eventually joins me, pulling my legs over his lap and absentmindedly massaging my feet, that I look up. The tree's standing tall, but the branches are bent in weird shapes, clinging close to the stem from being wrapped up tight in plastic. I've never had a real tree before, but this doesn't look right. "Is it supposed to be like that?"

Griffin chuckles as he passes Cole a beer and takes a seat on the sofa across from us. "It needs twenty-four hours to settle, then we can fluff it up and decorate it."

"You have decorations?"

"Why else would we get a tree?"

I lean my head against the armrest and hum as

Cole presses his thumb into my instep. "I guess I just didn't picture you as the tree-decorating type."

Griffin turns on the TV, switching it to a Bruins game before answering. "I like anything to do with spending time with my family."

My throat goes thick as his words settle in me. There's just the three of us here, and somehow, he's made me feel included in that.

Chapter 7

Eve

I'm not sure how long I've been reading, but the sun's already set when I look up.

Cole smiles at me. "Good book?"

My cheeks heat because there was more than one scene in it that had me squirming.

I clear my throat. "Hmmm? Really good."

He swipes his thumb over my bottom lip, freeing it from my teeth. "You'll have to read it for me someday."

Embarrassment takes over, but I can't deny it's enticing. Would he like the things I read? Would he be willing to do them with me?

From the way he's smirking, he knows exactly what happens in my books.

It takes several seconds for me to realize the hockey game is over and he's moved on to the Xbox. He has a controller in his hand, dangling from his fingers.

"Do you want to play?"

I shake my head. "No way. I'm horrible."

"That's half the fun." He looks up at me through his lashes, round eyes pleading. "Come on. Play with me."

I let out a breath, knowing there's no way I'm winning this. "Alright, but no making fun of me when I suck."

"I would never."

We'll see about that. I think he's underestimating just how bad I am.

We're five games in when Cole finally lets out the laugh he's been holding in.

I collapse back, my head connecting with the back of the sofa. "I warned you."

"Warned him of what?" Griffin says, entering the room. He has another few cans of beer he doles out to each of us.

I groan, covering my eyes with my hands. "That I suck at video games."

The feeling of a large presence leaning over me fills my senses, as the rich scent of forest fills my nose with each breath. The sensation of Cole at my side and Griffin over me has my head growing fuzzy.

Large, rough fingers wrap around my wrist and gently pull my hands away. "Let me help you kick his ass."

"What? How?" My brain is still fuzzy, but even in this state, what he's saying doesn't make sense.

Griffin glances at Cole. "Move over."

"I was here first," Cole argues, not budging.

They do their silent communication thing, somehow both knowing what happens next. I, on the other hand, gasp when Griffin slides his arms under me, one behind my back, the other beneath my knees, and lifts me into the air. He takes my seat on the sofa, settling me on his lap, facing the TV. I stiffen, worry traveling through me until my gut churns, but one glance at Cole has my nerves calming.

"Relax, he's a skilled teacher." He gently squeezes my thigh before holding his controller and turns back to the screen. "Let's go, old man."

Griffin's laugh reverberates through my back, his breath sending tingles down my spine as he speaks into my ear. "Hold on to my wrists."

I grip each of his thick wrists in each hand as he holds the remote nimbly.

"Like this?" I ask.

"That's it, Baby Girl."

Griffin's heat envelops me as the game starts. He shifts as he plays, moving with his player. When he leans forward, his thighs tense under my ass, and my core presses into *it*. I suck in a breath, and I swear I hear a low rumble from him. I go to lift myself, mortification setting in, but Griffin's elbows tighten around me, holding me in place. With each of his movements, the friction grows until my core is wet, and my clit aches to be touched. If I leaned over just a little, I'd be able to get what my body craves.

"Eve, are you paying attention?" Cole asks from beside me.

"What?" I rasp, feeling like I've been caught in the act.

The room fills with laughter. "You won. What were you thinking about that you were so lost in thought?"

I can feel my cheeks heat. There's no way I can answer that question honestly.

Griffin's fingers wrap around my waist as he lifts me to my feet. "Sounds like your girl's tired. Why don't you take her to bed?"

I sway on my feet, and Cole catches me easily. Why does everything they say sound so seductive?

Cole's deep eyes meet mine. "Is that it? Are you tired?" He brushes a strand of my hair behind my ear and whispers into it. "I don't think that's it."

I shiver, goose bumps rising where his breath touched me. I have no response, so I bury my face in his chest to hide the way I'm responding.

"I've got you," Cole says moments before hauling me over his shoulder and spanking my ass.

I squeak, breath caught in my throat. "What was that for?"

"You know what," he growls and moves through the space easily, going to our room despite supporting my weight.

Is he spanking me because of how I reacted to sitting on Griffin's lap? Could he tell everything that was happening to me? Guilt twists my stomach.

His hand soothes where it slapped my ass. "Let it go. We're here to have fun."

How does he do that? How does he always make me feel alright, even when I'm freaking out?

He enters our room, maneuvering me so my legs are wrapped around his waist and his hard cock presses against my core, finally giving me the friction I've needed.

I moan and dig my heels into his back as he shuts the door behind us.

"You liked beating me in the game, didn't you?" Cole says while stripping me, then turns and presses my back against the wall. His teeth run along the shell of my ear. "Griffin's a good teacher, isn't he? He's good with his hands."

All I can do is nod against his shoulder, my hips moving on their own.

Cole grips my chin, guiding me to look at him. "Good."

He takes my mouth in demanding kisses and rocks his cock against my core, making me gasp his name.

I struggle with his belt and clumsily undo his button.

"Tell me what you need." He pushes his pants down and lines the head of his cock with my core.

"I need you," I gasp as he enters me.

He grips my hair, pulling my head back. "I'll give you anything you want."

Chapter 8

Griffin

MY BACK'S against the wall as Cole fucks Eve on the other side. The vibration from their movements drives me crazy. I shouldn't be doing this, but there's no way I can stop. Not after she squirmed on my lap, nearly driving me insane. My cock presses painfully against my jeans, and I undo the button, freeing it, pushing the thick fabric and my boxers down my thighs. The head of my cock's already dripping with precum, just listening to them.

Each time she moans, my body tenses, wishing I was the reason she's making those sounds. I run my thumb along the slit, collecting the moisture before stroking down. My hand glides freely, and I groan, imagining her pussy clenching around me with each stroke. The way she'd moan as I thrust into her. Her nails dig into my shoulders until she leaves her mark. I want signs of her all over me, proof of her desire.

I want to leave my own marks, covering her with deep red hickeys and the imprint of my teeth. Fuck, I bet her nipples turn a rosy red, swelling as I suck on them. My hand moves faster with each thought, the sound of Cole fucking her coming clear through the wall.

Is he right? Will she accept both of us? Will she writhe under me as I take her hard?

My dick swells, precum leaking over my knuckles. I want to know how she tastes, how she reacts when my tongue pushes into her.

My body tenses, my grip growing firm, squeezing the head almost painfully, trying to hold off my orgasm just a little longer, but it's no use. She cries out Cole's name with her release, and I soak my shirt in spurts of cum.

My mind clears. I don't feel guilty for listening in on them, especially because I know Cole did it on purpose. All I can think about is getting her under me.

Now, we just need to convince her that she wants this as badly as we do.

From the way she responded to my touch, it's possible she already does.

I want to claim her as part of our family and never let her go.

Chapter 9

Eve

COLE RAISES the chairlift bar over our heads, and I swallow hard as I hop off the seat. Growing up in Florida, there weren't any opportunities to go skiing. So my only experience is going a few times on the smaller ski hill in Colorado near the college. The boys have assured me we'll be going down a green hill and I can do it.

Hesitantly, I follow them to the top of the hill, my heart racing in my chest, making it hard to breathe.

Cole removes his gloves and checks my helmet strap. "You okay?"

I meet his clear green eyes, and I know if I said I wasn't, he'd find a way to get me down this hill without me having to ski another foot.

Humiliation at the thought of being driven down

71

on a snowmobile has me telling him, "I'm good...just a little nervous."

He squeezes my arms. "We'll both be here with you the entire time. You're safe."

Safe...yeah, sure. Says the guy who's spent his entire life on the slopes, but still, his words give me a semblance of comfort.

"You ready, Baby Girl?" Griffin calls up from where he's perched sideways a dozen feet below us.

My chest tightens at the distance.

"Remember what we showed you. Point the tips of your skis together and your weight on your heels to slow you down," Cole reassures me. "I'll be right with you."

He moves so that he's in front of me, facing up the hill directly at me, and holds out his hands. "Come to me."

He's only a few feet ahead, alleviating some of the fear. I position my skis like they said and slowly make my way toward him. He's able to maintain his balance as he slides down the hill backward, never leaving too much space between us. We're a quarter of the way before I realize it, and my breathing has evened out.

Griffin comes up beside me. "You feeling better? What do you think about him giving you a little more room?"

I glance back to Cole, who's waiting patiently for

my answer, making it known he'll do whatever I want. Both men have made it abundantly clear that my comfort is their top priority.

I breathe out. "Okay."

Cole nods and slowly puts distance between us until there's a fifteen-foot gap. Fear crawls up my spine.

"You've got this. You already have control of your speed. Now we're just working on your confidence."

Realization that even though Cole's been in front of me this entire time, I've been the one slowing myself gives me a little boost. It's been me the entire time. They're just here to support.

"I've got this." I look down at my feet, which both Griffin and Cole warned me not to do, and lose the pizza shape of my skis.

I press hard on my heels, but I can't slow down. I'm approaching Cole faster and faster, but he doesn't move, like he's unafraid of me crashing into him.

Squeezing my eyes tight, I prepare myself for the fall, but Cole catches me easily.

He presses his helmet to mine. "See, I told you I have you."

My breaths come out hard, but none of it matters. I've never felt so safe in my life.

Griffin's firm hands wrap around me from behind. "How about you ski down the rest of the way with me?

Just keep your skis between mine, and I'll take care of the rest."

Even in the cold winter air, my skin heats in his arms. I crane my head back to see him. "Together?"

"Yeah, just trust me and relax."

Trust him. Cole's giving me a warm smile, and Griffin's arms tighten, holding me close.

"I trust you."

Griffin makes a satisfied sound in the back of his throat, sending tingles down my neck, and shifts so that we're moving down the hill much faster than I had been.

Fear trails through me at first, but he puts me at ease. Each of his movements is controlled and trained, like his skis are a part of him. All I have to do is lean back.

The wind whips around me as we descend, and a bubbling sensation fills my chest until my smile turns into a laugh.

I'm having so much fun I'm almost disappointed when we reach the bottom.

I spin around to them. Both men wear matching smiles.

"Again?"

Chapter 10

Cole

I REST against the corner of the hot tub, letting the jets massage my back. Muscles I haven't used this year ache all over. Griffin's on the other side, eyes closed as he relaxes in the hot water. I'm about to ask him how he's feeling about the progress we've made with Eve when the sliding door opens, and my breath catches in my throat. She's standing there in a bright pink bikini, her breasts overflowing the triangles of her top. I want to bite every inch of her. The desire to eat her up is overwhelming.

"I should have tried it on before bringing it." She's fidgeting on her feet like she's uncomfortable, and I hate everything about it. My girl should never feel anything but perfect.

I raise my brows, ready to correct her, but Griffin says, "What are you talking about? You look delicious."

His eyes are hooded, teeth biting into his lips, completely unaware of just how inappropriate what he said is.

I watch Eve for any signs that she's uncomfortable, but there's only a flush crawling up her neck.

"Get in here before you freeze and catch a cold," I say, taking her hand as I guide her over the edge and pull her into my lap, enjoying the way her soft skin feels against my chest. I doubt she wants me to fuck her right here, but I'm not sure how I'm going to control myself.

Eve's stiff, her back rigid as she soaks between us as if she doesn't know what to do with herself. I massage my thumbs on her shoulders, pressing upward in gentle circles. Her body loosens instantly with my touch, and her head rolls forward to give me better access.

"You must be sore," I say, working my way down her back.

She hums. "That feels good."

I look at Griffin. His gaze is nearly pitch-black as he takes her in. He's focused on the way the water skims the swells of her breasts, leaving them half-exposed. His eyes meet mine, the hunger clear as day. He needs to touch her as badly as I do.

Wrapping my hand around her throat, I guide Eve's head up to face me. "Let us help you."

Her gaze darts to Griffin's, then back to mine, and her voice comes out in a squeak. "Both of you?"

I give her a reassuring smile. "Griffin's good at this. It'll feel good."

Griffin doesn't hesitate to move forward and take one of her feet into his hands, kneading the arch in slow, controlled movements before switching to the other.

Eve's back arches in response before her eyes close and she gives in, completely at our mercy as we touch her all over. I slide my hands around her front and graze the underside of her breast with my knuckles. She squirms in my hold but doesn't pull away. Her heartbeat pounds, skipping like crazy as Griffin and I massage her.

Griffin moves closer, gripping her calves and squeezing them. He takes his time working his way upward, and she moans when he wraps his hands around her thighs.

I turn my lips against her ear. "That feel good? You want to keep going?"

She nods, panting, each breath coming out faster than the last.

My fingers graze the seam of her bikini bottoms, and her stomach hollows out, body going rigid in my hands.

"Breathe. Concentrate on how you feel." She sucks

79

in a breath, and I dip my fingers beneath the fabric, circling her clit.

Her hips buck, and Griffin holds them in place, keeping her thighs open for me.

She's vibrating and bites down hard on her lip as I dip two fingers into her and press my palm into her clit. She swallows her cries as I bring her to orgasm, kissing up her throat.

Griffin moves back to his side of the hot tub. "Feel better, Baby Girl?"

Chapter 11

Eve

"SEE YOU IN THE MORNING, you two." Griffin calls it a night and disappears into his room as Cole follows me into ours.

Mortification rolls through me after what just happened. Did I really let Cole get me off in front of Griffin? Could he tell what was happening? Who am I kidding? Of course he could. At least the water was dark enough he couldn't actually see Cole's hand. I grip my towel to cover my face.

I can't believe I did that.

I can't believe Cole was okay with that. Not only okay with it but actively encouraged it.

I meet his gaze, worried about what I'll see there, but he just gives me a lopsided grin and tries to follow me into the bathroom.

"Oh no you don't." I quickly shut the door between us. "Go shower somewhere else."

He laughs low in his throat. "Fine. I'll use Griffin's. Take your time."

Grateful my hair isn't too wet, I clean off with soap that smells like Cole. The memory of their hands on me, how each of them gripped my body, takes control of my brain. Even now, I can feel heat growing between my thighs. I don't know what's gotten into me, but I can't control myself as I slide my fingers over my core and pinch my nipple. It feels fantastic, but not enough. I need more, and I need it now.

I get out of the shower, grabbing the white, fluffy robe. Quietly as possible, I sneak through the hall into the living area, spotting Cole sitting at the table. I scan the area.

"*Fuck.* Have I ever told you how lucky I am that you're my girl?" His eyes are dark as he runs his hands up the back of my legs, sending shivers along their path.

I grip his hair and tug his head back. "Take me to bed."

Cole groans, lifting from his seat, and swoops me onto the table and stands between my thighs.

My eyes go wide, and I shake my head. "What are you doing? We can't do this here."

"Sure we can. We're alone." His mouth descends on mine, taking away the last of my rational thoughts, and he kisses me until my lungs burn and I turn to Jell-O at his touch.

He leans back, biting his lower lip as he touches the robe belt and slowly undoes it. "Do I get to unwrap my present now?"

I'm practically vibrating as his mouth follows the path. He licks down my neck, nipping at my collarbone before descending to my chest, sucking the nipple hard until I arch into his mouth, gasping. He has control of every one of my senses, and I don't want it back. His lips travel down my stomach, stopping to swirl his tongue around my navel before he rocks back on his heels and looks at me, laid out naked in front of him.

Cole's hands slide down my thighs, separating them further apart, leaving me completely exposed. I try to close them, but he lowers, running his tongue along my clit. My moan breaks free at his touch, and he does it again. I'm lost to him, not caring what happens next, just needing more of what he's offering.

I grip his hair, pushing him into me.

He chuckles, licking up my seam before sliding two fingers into my core, stretching me around them.

The back of my head pushes into the table as he moves them in and out. There's a noise at the end of the room that catches my attention.

I jerk, spotting Griffin at the door. He's shirtless, wearing only a pair of low-slung jogging pants. My heart slams against my rib cage with each second he lingers. I swallow hard when instead of leaving, he takes a step forward. My mind's rebelling against me. I know I should be embarrassed, mortified. I know I should scream at Griffin to leave. To cover myself up.

A frantic sound escapes my throat as my pulse rushes in my ears. Nothing about what's happening makes sense.

Cole's firm grip holds me in place and draws my attention back to him. He kisses my knee, and a calmness settles over me as he anchors me in this moment. As long as he's looking at me like that, with soft, hooded eyes and a warm smile, I know everything will be okay.

He presses his lips to my skin, then bites the spot gently as he resumes the seductive pace of his fingers, stroking in and out.

"Do you want Griffin to see how pretty your pussy is when it's wet like this? How it turns a deep pink and your clit swells when you're turned on?" Cole runs his thumb over my clit, meeting my gaze. "Look how he's watching us, how badly he wants to see you."

Griffin's eyes are hooded, muscles strained as he trails his tongue over his bottom lip. He looks like an animal ready to devour me.

Heat floods me, and my back arches against the table. The way both men are watching me is almost more than I can take.

My pussy pulses, and Cole kisses my knee again. "Do you want him to see?"

I nod, breath caught in my throat, and watch as Griffin comes around the table, muscle ticking in his jaw as Cole spreads my legs wider.

Embarrassment courses through me, and I cover my face, but it doesn't stop the sound of Cole's soaked fingers entering me from reaching my ears.

"Don't hide. I want to see every single reaction as Cole touches you. While he makes you feel good. Can you do that for me, Baby Girl?" Thick fingers wrap around my wrist and slowly uncover my eyes.

"Such a good girl," Griffin tells me, voice low and gravelly, before gazing down to where Cole spreads my legs further as he kisses his way down to my pussy.

We all groan when he licks a path through my slit, lifting my hips higher so he can thrust his tongue into my core.

Griffin grips his cock through his jogging pants, and I desperately want to see it. I glimpsed it when I accidentally walked into his room, and I need to know if it's as big as I remember.

"You want to taste her, don't you?" Cole asks, running his tongue over my clit.

"Fuck," Griffin moans.

"What about you, Eve? Do you want him to taste you?" Cole looks so turned on it makes me want to let go and just chase the pleasure. "We won't do anything you're not comfortable with. But don't worry about me." He bites the inside of my thigh. "This is hot as fuck."

There's no jealousy, only lust in his voice. It feels like permission. *Acceptance.* For the first time in my life, I can have everything that I want.

He thrusts his fingers back inside and curls them, hitting that sensitive spot. "I'll ask again. Do you want him to taste you?"

I nod, craving it.

Cole shakes his head. "This time, I need you to use your words."

"Yes."

"Yes, what?"

"I want him to...taste me," I beg.

Griffin growls, and they switch places so he's between my thighs, his hot breath against my core. He's more aggressive when he takes me, mouth devouring every inch, humming as he licks a path up my seam. "You taste so good. I could drown in you."

I gasp when his tongue buries inside me, filling me over and over before he replaces it with his fingers. My brain goes fuzzy as my nerves come alive at his touch.

His palm is rough on my thigh as he holds me open, devouring me thoroughly until I'm calling out his name and begging him for something I can't even understand. The only rational thought I have is that I need more. More of him. More of *them.*

Griffin flattens his tongue against my clit before sucking on it as his fingers curl, pressing that deep, sensitive spot within me. Any last thought I'd been holding on to shatters under what this man is doing to me.

I wrap my trembling legs around his back, no longer able to hold them up on my own. Tension builds as shivers travel through my body, coiling as Griffin drives me higher and higher until it feels like I can touch the sky before he drops me down and lets my orgasm suck me under.

I'm shaking as my orgasm pulses through me for what feels like minutes instead of moments.

The back of my head drops to the table as I struggle to inhale.

Griffin wipes his face, then sucks his fingers into his mouth, moaning around them.

It's so hot that it goes against the laws of physics— even after that mind-bending orgasm, my body craves more.

Griffin steps away, letting Cole replace him between my thighs.

My boyfriend's clear green eyes stare down at me with lust as he runs the tip of his cock along my entrance. "You are soaked for us. So ready to take my cock."

He slowly fills me until he bottoms out.

Griffin grips my thigh, pulling it wider, and looks down to where his stepson and I are connected. "You take him so well, Baby Girl."

The veins in Griffin's forearm stand out. How can someone's forearm be so hot?

He pushes down his pants and fists the tip of his cock. His thighs flex as he strokes himself faster, the tip growing wet with precum. My heart's racing in my chest, a heavy lust rushing through my veins, heading straight to my core. It practically begs me to touch it. He's staring at me with dark eyes, not looking away as he fucks his hand.

I dig my nails into Cole's hands, where they grip my hips as he thrusts harder into me, leading me closer and closer to the edge.

"Your pussy's clenching around me," Cole grunts, slamming into me, his hot gaze on mine. "Come for us, Eve."

With his words, I'm coming again. This time, it's all-consuming. Like it's being ripped through me, body and soul, as my release takes over me.

"That's it. Come for us," Cole says, filling me with spurts of hot liquid.

Griffin collapses, his head landing on my knee moments after he covers my chest with his cum.

"Fuck, Baby Girl. How are you so perfect?"

Cole disappears into the kitchen while I'm still trying to catch my breath. I'm too tired to examine what just happened.

Instead, I let the warm, tingling feeling fill my heavy limbs.

Griffin's tracing small, calming circles as he brushes my hair back, helping me calm enough to catch my breath.

Cole returns with a wet washcloth and cleans me in gentle strokes, taking extra care around my sensitive clit. My blinks slow as sleep takes me over, the events of today exhausting me.

I'll think about all this tomorrow. For tonight, I lean on Cole as he lifts me into his arms and brings me to our room, lowering me to the bed. He ditches the rest of his clothes, climbing into bed beside me and tugging me close in his arms.

He kisses my temple, pushing my hair behind my ear. "I love you so fucking much."

His words swirl around my heart, filling it until it feels like it'll burst. After so long of feeling unlovable, this man has worked his way through my broken chest and put it back together, piece by piece.

Tears pool at the corner of my eyes, and my voice wavers.

"I love you too."

Chapter 12

Eve

"TIME TO GET UP," Cole says as he presses a kiss to my temple.

I roll over, lifting the covers over my head. I'm still tired from yesterday, and I don't want to face what we did in the light of day. What if I read Cole wrong? What if he felt pressured into doing it? What if he's actually mad at me?

He wraps me in his arms, squeezing me. "We have a fun day planned."

Some of my worries ease out of me with his touch, and I peel the cover back to reveal my face. "What kind of thing?"

"The fun kind. Come on. Dress warm. I double promise you're going to like it."

I groan, still sore from yesterday. "It's not skiing again, is it?"

Cole laughs, the vibration traveling through me. "Something even better."

"Fine. But I reserve the right to back out." My stomach growls, and my cheeks heat.

"Food first. Got it," he smirks.

I push him off me. "Shower first."

His eyes darken as if he's remembering exactly what we did yesterday.

"Can I join you?"

"Not a freaking chance."

I take a while to shower and blow-dry my hair. My chest tightens at the idea that they're out there waiting for me. I've been told my entire life I'm nothing but a nuisance, and the thought they may feel the same has me rushing through getting ready.

The thoughts are wiped away by giddiness.

Cole loves me.

Feeling a little more confident, I dress in leggings and a long-sleeve shirt, pulling on thick wool socks. A quick glance in the mirror has me freezing in place. Normally I'd be self-conscious about how I look, with every curve and roll revealed, but somehow, after last night, I've gained a little more confidence.

As expected, they're waiting for me in the kitchen, both holding coffees, steam rising from the tops.

Cole turns toward me and gives me a lopsided smile. "As always, you're worth the wait."

"Sorry. I shouldn't have washed my hair." I run my fingers through the thick locks, trying to hide the way they tremble. "It takes too long to dry it."

Cole's at my side in an instant and tugs gently at the end. "Never apologize for making me wait. It makes me feel good that you like to dress up for me."

Warmth wraps around my chest, swirling beneath my rib cage, and I drop my forehead to his chest, letting him pull me into a hug. He slides his hand up and down my back in gentle strokes, patiently waiting for me. I pull back and look behind us, only to see that Griffin's looking away. His knuckles are tight around his mug. His face is turned downward, and there's a slight pink crawling up the back of his neck.

Flashes from last night come pummeling into my brain. His touch, his tongue, how he stroked himself so vividly in my memory that heat pools between my thighs. Now that it's morning and everything is clear, does he regret it? Regretting it didn't even cross my mind, but by the way he can't even look at me, I feel like he does. The back of my throat tightens, and my eyes burn.

I must make a sound because he finally looks up. His brows pull together, and the corners of his eyes crinkle. He stands, taking a step toward me, then freezes. "I pushed you too far last night. I'm sorry, I never meant to make you...uncomfortable."

Cole squeezes my shoulder in reassurance as I tilt my head to the side. Griffin's standing in front of me, worry clearly written across his face, as if he's just waiting for me to crush him. I close the distance between us and hold his face in my hands, lifting on my toes and pressing my mouth to his.

A low hum rumbles through him as his arms wrap around me, tugging me closer and deepening the kiss.

My heart is pounding wildly in my chest. "Does that feel like I regret it?"

He drops his head to mine. "Fuck. How are you so perfect?"

I bite the corner of my lip. "There's nothing perfect about me."

His eyes narrow. "I'm going to make sure you never think like that again."

"Alright, you two. Break it up, we have places to go," Cole says, still standing where I left him. I search his face to see if there's any jealousy there. Anything to show he's upset about what just happened.

He's grinning at us, eyes gleaming. "If we don't get out of here now, I can't promise I won't drag you back into bed and never let you out."

Griffin's arm bands around my back. "I kind of like the sound of that."

"Later. We need to give her a rest before tonight."

He grabs his hoodie from the chair and walks over to us, pulling it over my head.

I pop through, loving the fact that I swim in it like a dress. "What's tonight?"

Cole swipes his thumb over my bottom lip. "Presents."

———

Cole's talking to his friend who owns this mushing team. Apparently, he set up this little meet and greet before we came to the cabin, knowing it was something I'd enjoy.

A soft, wet nose presses against my palm. This is better than anything I could've expected. We've been surrounded by huskies of all different colors for the last few hours, and they all want pets. Today's their day off work, so it's their certified spa day. Cole had been nervous when we first got here at the idea of putting me to work, but I jumped into feeding, washing, and brushing the puppies' coats.

I smile up at Griffin, who's already looking at me.

"You look happy," he says.

"I am." I'm not paying attention, so I don't notice one of the larger dogs jump up for a hug, and I tumble backward under its weight.

"Woah. I've got you." Strong arms catch me, wrapping around my middle. Griffin's chin presses into my neck. "Your heart's beating like crazy."

I swallow hard. "Of course it is. Look at the way you're holding me."

Griffin's grip tightens where his thumb grazes the underside of my breast over the quilted fabric of my coat I threw on over Cole's sweater. I shiver in response. The desire to have that hand inch up just a little more has me pushing back into him.

Cole comes jogging toward us. "So, what do you think of your surprise?"

I push down the worry that he won't like what I brought him. "Best surprise ever, but what present were you talking about tonight?"

"Oh, that's completely different," Griffin adds. "Let's get some lunch before heading back."

Chapter 13

Eve

Cole rubs his hand up and down my side, pulling me closer. He'd decided we'd sit together in the back seat because, according to him, we haven't had enough cuddle time. I should have seen it for the setup that it is. My boyfriend's using this opportunity to drive me insane with his stepdad so close in the front seat.

He runs his teeth along the curve of my ear before sucking on the bottom. "Let me make you feel good."

Heat floods through me with his words and the way his breath fans out over my neck. I twist in my seat to kiss him, but he pulls me over his lap so my back is to his chest and buckles us together.

"Safety first." His hand runs under my jacket and up my stomach, not stopping until he grips my breast, drawing a moan from my lips. I glance up to where

Griffin watches us through the rearview mirror until he's forced to look back at the road.

"Doing that without me is a cruel form of torture," he murmurs from the front seat.

Cole unzips my jacket and lifts my sweater. "Do you want me to stop?"

"Just make her feel good."

"Yes, sir," Cole replies, reaching down between my thighs, grinding his palm against my clit. My core clenches, wanting more.

He slips his hand below my bra and pinches my nipple hard enough that I gasp, my head falling back to his shoulder.

"Like that?" Cole asks, and Griffin replies with a grunt.

"Stop teasing her and make it quick. We're almost home."

"How about you? Do you want me to touch you?" Cole asks, already knowing the answer.

"Please," I beg.

"You hear our girl?" Cole slips his fingers under my bottoms and groans. "She's already soaked."

"Tell me," Griffin commands.

Cole enters me with two fingers, stroking them back and forth. "She's taking my fingers so well."

Their words have me losing control, pressing my hips forward, chasing the feeling of Cole's hand.

I gasp as his movements quicken. My core clenches as Cole gives a play-by-play of everything we're doing and presses down on the sensitive spot inside me with each stroke.

I cry out, calling their names.

"Fuck," Griffin says from the front and pulls off to the side of the road. He turns back to us. "Let me see her."

Cole doesn't hesitate and pushes my clothes down to my ankles, spreading my knees wide so they hang on either side of his.

"See how her greedy pussy takes my fingers?" Cole says, filling me again.

I can't hold back from chanting their names as pleasure courses in my veins.

Griffin moves closer, the seats the only thing holding him back from getting to us. "Add another one. I want to see you stretch her."

It's Cole's turn to groan as he adds a third. The pressure builds with each of his movements, and my breath catches in my lungs until my head goes fuzzy.

"Look at me, Baby Girl."

My gaze snaps to Griffin, who's watching me with hunger. "You're doing such a good job. Your pussy is dripping all over him."

I moan, and Cole presses his palm into my clit, not slowing down.

"Make her come all over your hand, Cole."

Cole pinches my nipple and curls his fingers inside me, sending pleasure rippling between my thighs. I cry out as my orgasm crashes through me. Cole doesn't stop until he's pulled out every last drop.

I'm helpless, unable to move myself, as Cole lifts my pants and pulls my sweater down, covering me. His cock's rock hard beneath me, but he stops my hands when I go to release him.

I'm still lost in my afterglow when he kisses my temple, then tucks my head under his chin. "This was just for you."

Griffin pulls back onto the road as if nothing happened, like watching his stepson getting a girl off in the back seat is a regular occurrence. A twisting feeling turns my gut. What if this is normal for them?

I stop myself before I can spiral down that path. Whatever this is, it's only for the next few days, and then Cole and I will be returning to college. No use dissecting it. Somehow, that thought makes me feel worse than before.

Snow's falling as we pull up to the cabin, the sky a soft gray. There are already several inches accumulated on the stairs. I grip the railing, taking my time up the slippery wood, when Griffin lifts me in the air and cradles me against his chest.

"What are you doing?" I ask.

He raises a brow as if the answer is obvious. "Making sure you're safe."

"I'm not a kid. I can walk on my own."

He shrugs. "I know, but I needed an excuse to touch you."

Cole comes up behind us and tugs on my hair. "Come on. Let him do what he wants. It makes him feel needed."

I'm normally the one that feels out of place, so the idea of this big man feeling anything but wanted has my arms wrapping around his neck. "Anything for you, Daddy."

Griffin groans, and Cole laughs.

"You're killing me here," Griffin says, tightening his grip.

Chapter 14

Griffin

I SET Eve down on the sofa and tuck a blanket around her.

"You don't have to do this." I hate the way she sounds so insecure, like she really doesn't want to inconvenience me. God, if she only knew how much I want her to lean on me. She has no idea how badly I want her to be under my care.

"Trust me. I want to do this...*more* than this."

Her eyes go round, and her pretty pink lips fall open, making it hard to resist kissing her, but I haven't calmed down from the car yet, and there's no way I could control myself.

Cole walks in with a large plastic box, breaking the moment. "It's a bit late, but look what I've got!"

I watch Eve as he places the box on the table. Her face lights up and eyes gleam when she spots what's inside. It's packed full of every type of Christmas orna-ment you can think of, and the sheer giddiness on her face makes it worth dragging that tree in here.

She's digging through the decorations, pulling out her favorites, then pauses. "Are you sure it's okay for me to pick? This seems like a tradition of yours."

"It is a tradition. One we'd like you to be a part of." I clear my throat and look away when she tilts her head, trying to sort out my words. If she wasn't so down on herself, she'd be able to figure out exactly what I meant.

Eve lifts on her toes, reaching to place the bulb as high as possible, causing her shirt to rise up her back. A band of delicious golden skin that looks good enough to taste has me moving toward her.

I slide my hand across her back, hooking my thumb below her shirt, giving in to the need to touch her. My cock twitches as she shivers, still not soft since watching Cole get her off in the car. It damn near killed me to stay in the front seat and not fuck her right there. The only thing holding me back is we want our first time to mean something, for her to feel as safe and wanted as possible, and that's not going to happen in the back seat of a Range Rover. Not to say it'll never happen in the future.

I kiss the top of Eve's head. "Let me help you with that."

She goes to hand me the bulb, but I brush away her hand, lifting her in the air and over my shoulders.

"Are you crazy! I'm way too heavy for this," she squeals.

I squeeze her thigh and chuckle. "Don't insult me. You barely weigh anything."

She grips my hair when I hop in place, showing off my point.

"Okay! Okay! Don't move." She leans in and hooks the blue bulb onto a branch.

"Here's another one." Cole hands her a red bulb this time. His arms are full of decorations of all kinds.

She takes it and adds it to the tree. "Are we really going to do this until it's done? Won't you two get tired?"

"I'm not sure if that's an insult to our stamina, but I'll be happy to show you just how long we can go once it's done," Cole says, and Eve's legs squeeze around my head.

The desire to lay her out and fuck her right here is almost more than I can take, but her smile as she continues to cover the tree keeps me in check.

Later. Later, I'll show my Baby Girl just how badly I want her.

Wash away any of that insecurity she tries to hide so desperately.

I meet Cole's gaze. He's wearing a knowing smile

as he glances between our girl and me. He wants this as badly as I do. Now, we just need to get Eve on board.

Eve ruffles my hair, grabbing my attention. "All done up here. You can let me down now."

A quick glance shows the entire top of the tree is finished, including the star, and I grumble as I lift her off my shoulders. I'd have been happy to keep her up there all day. Keeping her tight to my chest, every inch of her grazes me as she slides down to her feet. I groan as her ass presses back into my cock, stealing the blood from my head.

Her heart pounds against my chest, and I slowly turn her to face me. I want to see exactly what she's thinking before going further. Her wide doe eyes blink, and her pretty rose mouth is slightly ajar as she struggles to take in breaths. I feel frozen, caught in her gaze, following the path of her blush. I lean down until our mouths nearly meet and stroke my thumb over her pinkened cheek. The air grows thick and time stills as I move in closer, stealing the space between us.

Her lips are soft and warm as I take them with mine, not hesitating to deepen the kiss when she gasps for breath. I kiss her until I've stolen the air from her lungs and the thoughts from her head, not allowing her to hesitate about a single thing we're doing.

Cole comes up behind her and kisses along the

back of her neck, up to her ear. "You look amazing right now."

It must be the right thing to reassure her because she arches, reaching an arm back to twist around and kiss him, and presses her hips against me.

I grab Cole's arms and tug him closer until she's sandwiched between us and run my hands along her waist and up her shirt while she's busy kissing him.

She moans when I capture her nipple through her bra with my mouth. I suck her tender skin until the thin fabric is soaked before moving on to the next one.

Her hips jerk, and she grips my hair as I pull the cup down, taking her into my mouth, wrapping my tongue against her swollen peak.

I hum deep in my throat and grip one of her thighs, lifting it so it wraps around my hips. She immediately grinds herself into us. "That's it, Baby Girl. Take what you need."

Her head falls back to Cole's shoulder, and he runs kisses up the side of her neck. Her eyes are closed, mouth open as I watch them. Cole meets my gaze before whispering. My heart pounds in my chest, knowing this is the moment that will change everything, whether that's for better or worse.

"For Christmas, I want to watch Griffin have sex with you. To know just how good your pussy feels wrapped around his cock. Better yet, I want you to take us both."

His words send a shiver through her, and I don't breathe until she nods, her heel digging into my back, pulling me closer.

It's like a dam breaks inside me. Our girl has no idea what she's just agreed to, but I'm going to make her crave every second.

Chapter 15

Eve

MY BRAIN's fuzzy as Cole's words process through me and send heat flooding my core. I want it so badly; it feels impossible to be true. To feel myself pressed between them. To have them both taking me is something I couldn't have imagined in my wildest dreams. I've grown closer to both of them this week. I had no idea it was possible to open my heart to two men, but I can't deny that's what happened. I love Cole. He's always given me everything I've wanted, and this is no different.

I turn to search his face, checking that this is what he really wants.

He smiles down at me. "Please. I want to feel you between us."

His darkened gaze and pleading words let me

know he wants this as badly as I do. I strip off my shirt in response, reaching back and unclasping my bra.

Cole ducks his head, taking my breast into his mouth as he pushes my leggings and panties to the ground. I'm naked between them, but their warm hands heat my skin as they both cover every inch of me. Cole kisses a path down my stomach as he drops to his knees.

He looks up at me through his lashes as he lifts my thigh over his shoulder, moving me so close his breath fans over my core. He doesn't break away from my gaze as he runs his tongue along my slit, groaning deep in his throat.

"Always so fucking delicious."

My knees go weak, and Griffin bands his thick arm around my stomach as his rough hand pinches and tweaks my nipple. The simultaneous sensations are almost too much to take.

My core stretches around Cole's fingers as he pushes them deep inside me, his movements painfully slow for what I need.

There's a sound of a zipper, then the feeling of Griffin's hot cock pressing against my ass between us. I press back, wanting nothing more than for him to fill me. My body trembles with anticipation as both men tease me—Cole with his slow movements and Griffin with the way his dick is so close, but he's not giving me what I want.

I let out a needy, pleading sound, and Griffin's laugh is a hot huff on my neck. "Call me Daddy and I'll give you what you need."

The pleasure that runs through me is almost enough to make me come. "Please, Daddy. Please fuck me."

He groans loudly.

Cole pulls his mouth off, leaving my clit, but he's not looking up at me. Instead, he reaches between us and guides Griffin's tip to my entrance. "Fuck, I want to see how pretty you are stretched around him."

Griffin doesn't wait, pushing fully inside me. He's too big, filling me completely and bringing tears to my eyes. I almost back out, but Cole's mouth covers my clit, sucking hard, turning any pain into pleasure.

Dual pleasure takes over. Both of them drive me closer to the edge until I'm plummeting into my release.

I cry out, gripping Cole's hair, holding him in place until they've pulled every last ounce of pleasure out of me, but it's still not enough.

Griffin pauses, giving me a second to catch my breath. "Feel good, Baby Girl? Can you take a little more?"

I need them so badly it's nearly killing me. "Yes, I need more."

"Good girl," Griffin says as he pushes down on my shoulders, bending me forward.

Cole's standing, his pants and shirt pulled off, looking down at me. His hard cock is between us, gently brushing against my lips, and my mouth grows wet with the need to taste him. Cole's jaw is clenched tight like he's using every muscle to stop himself from forcing his way inside me.

I run my tongue along his slit, licking his precum and enjoying the way he trembles at my touch. A part of me wants to torture him forever, but I know there's no way Griffin's going to remain patient. I wrap my mouth around Cole's cock, humming as I take him in.

He moans as I lick along the bottom of his head, his hips jerking forward, forcing me to swallow around him.

Griffin's hands tighten on my hips as he thrusts his cock into me, filling me from both ends. I dig my nails into Cole's legs, trying to keep myself upright as I take both men. I moan, and Cole grips my hair, pushing deeper as Griffin's hips slap against my ass.

There's a power that surges through me, knowing I'm the one that's making them lose control. Spit covers my chin as I gag, taking them both, loving the way they each pound into me.

Cole's cock swells in my mouth, and he groans. "I'm close."

Griffin slams into me, chasing his own orgasm as he reaches under me and circles fingers over my clit. The pleasure is overwhelming as hot cum fills my mouth, and my orgasm crashes over me like a wave, pulling me under. Griffin groans, covering my back with his hot release before pulling me into his arms and dropping his head between my shoulder blades.

"You were made for us."

Our breaths mingle as his words sink in, and I drop my forehead to his collarbone to stop them from seeing me. There's a sliver of pain running down my chest, knowing this is only temporary. Guilt curdles in my stomach at the thought that Cole's not enough for me anymore. How could I ever tell him that?

Warm arms wrap around my back, and Cole's low voice soothes me. "Just breathe and trust us. We've got you."

I desperately want that to be true.

Chapter 16

Eve

I SNUGGLE DEEPER into the warmth, face pressed against something both hard and soft, breathing in the scent of sandalwood. Exhaling, I open my eyes to see Cole already looking down at me.

"Morning. Merry Christmas"

"Merry Christmas." Warmth builds in my chest just as a yawn takes over. "I think I could've slept another six hours."

"Were we too rough on you yesterday?" Griffin's hot breath fans along the back of my neck as he places gentle kisses along the tender skin.

Cole brushes his knuckles over my cheeks. "Look at you blushing so pretty for us."

A very naked Griffin presses his length against my back. "Let us help get you back to sleep."

Cole kisses me while Griffin's hands explore,

lighting up every cell of my body. I'm gasping for breath by the time Cole takes my nipple into his mouth, and one of their hands descends between my thighs.

A phone rings on the night table, and I turn to get it.

Griffin gently bites my shoulder. "Just ignore it."

I try. I really do, but after the call ends, they just call again, finally breaking all of my concentration.

Griffin groans, turning over, and grabs his phone. "Something better be on fire."

Cole's soft chuckle reverberates through me as he tucks me against his chest. "I'd hate to be whoever's on the other end of that call."

It's not until Griffin goes quiet, listening carefully, that I realize something is really happening. I check his face, praying nothing tragic happened, but he looks frustrated, not sad.

"I'll be there in a few hours. Don't fuck it up before I get there," he says and hangs up the phone.

Griffin leans over and places a gentle kiss on my temple. "I've got to go to work, Baby Girl. There's a critical emergency at work I have to take care of."

My ribs constrict around my lungs, but I put on a smile, not wanting either man to see how I'm feeling. This has always been the plan. It's just happening a day early.

It doesn't take long for Griffin to pack up his stuff and drop his bags at the door before turning to me. His brows are pulled low over his eyes, his mouth together in a thin line.

My throat grows thick, and the back of my eyes sting as I fight down this growing feeling.

He reaches out to me. "Come here."

I take a step toward him, and he wraps me in a bear hug, tucking my head into his chest.

"I hate leaving you, Baby Girl. I don't want to say goodbye."

A small sob escapes my mouth before I can stop it, and he cups my face, pulling it back so he can see me. He swipes his thumbs under my eyes, catching my tears. "Don't cry. I promise it'll be okay."

For his reassurance, he doesn't let me go for several minutes, as if he doesn't want to leave as much as I want him to stay. His lips take mine in a deep kiss that takes over my every thought.

It's Cole who finally breaks us up, wrapping his arms around me and pulling me into his chest. "I've got her."

"You better," Griffin replies, then takes one last look at me before walking out the door.

Pain radiates through my chest, stealing my ability to breathe properly. I just want to curl up into a ball and pull the covers over my head.

"It's okay. I've got you." Cole sits me up and takes his time helping me dress. My legs feel weak as he lifts me off the ground, cradling me in his arms, and sits us on the living room couch. He runs his hands through my hair quietly until I've calmed down.

"I'm sorry. I don't know why I'm reacting this way." I sniff and stare up at the light, trying to stop the tears that threaten to overflow my lashes.

Cole kisses my forehead. "I'm sad too. What do you say if we head home tonight instead?"

I nod, half hating that it's over, half glad that I don't have to spend any more time here. How can it feel like everything just clicked into place to have it all snap apart a moment later?

I need to pull myself together before Cole's feelings get hurt. It's not like he offered to open up our relationship permanently.

I wipe my face with my sleeves and force a smile. "I'm just being sappy after we've been doing so much. A little fresh air and my own bed will make everything better."

Cole hums low in his throat, then lifts me onto my feet. "First, let's start packing, then we can grab breakfast on the way out. Get you back before you know it."

He looks worried as he watches me with soft eyes.

"Sounds perfect." I lift on my toes and kiss him. The

absolute last thing I want is for him to feel bad about anything that happened this weekend. I'll always hold it as a special memory, something to think of now and then, but I won't let him be sad about how things turned out.

The drive's slow and quiet. Soft music playing through the radio keeps us company. I'd be worried there was something wrong if it wasn't for the way Cole's hand cups my thigh and his thumb draws small, soothing circles against my skin. We've been off the mountain roads for a while, and I already miss the giant evergreens that take up the sky.

Now the freeway I've never really noticed feels cold and sterile in comparison. I'm watching cars pass by when Cole turns off at an unexpected exit.

"My stop's not for another two overpasses. Did you go on autopilot? This one goes to the school." I laugh under my breath, the first bit of lightness since this morning.

Cole squeezes my thigh. "I thought we'd go somewhere else first."

Streets pass by, then turn to residential until we're pulling in front of a multistory brick home.

My gaze flashes to Cole. "Whose house is this?"

He turns off the engine and smiles at me. "This is where I stay when I'm not at my apartment."

Embarrassment forms in my gut. Why did we spend so much time at my low-income apartment when he had this place so close to school?

"What are we doing here?" I ask, intimidated by the size and the grandeur of his home but also not wanting to go home by myself. Exhaustion has been hanging over me for hours, and I'm barely holding on.

"Come on. Trust me." Cole gets out and walks around the car, opening the door, and holds out his hand to me. "I promise this is a good thing."

Taking his hand, I let him lead me up to the front door, punching in the code like he's done this a million times before.

Cole smiles at me, and the warmth washes my worries away. If I just keep following him, everything will be alright.

The space is nicer than I even imagined. Towering ceilings, with a large chandelier hanging in the middle. The furniture is masculine, with tan leather couches and charcoal paneled walls. The darker color palette somehow makes the large space feel cozy. I'm still gazing at the open-concept layout when a low, deep voice rumbles from the other room. There's a familiarity to it that draws my attention, my heart skipping in my chest. I tamp it down, knowing that there's no way it can be who I'm thinking of. That Griffin's gone to some meeting he couldn't escape, but I can't help the way the air catches in my lungs as the man draws nearer.

Griffin's enormous frame enters through the hallway, head tilted down as he looks over paperwork while talking on the phone, and time stands still. He looks different from what he did on the mountain, his hair styled back, dressed in a black knitted sweater over charcoal dress pants. Gone is my rough-around-the-edges man, replaced with the crispness of professionalism. It feels like there's a distance between us now that we're here. Like that was all play, and this is reality. I blink away the tears pooling in my eyes. This is how it was always supposed to be.

"You really not going to say hi?" Cole says from behind me. His voice is as playful as ever.

I almost turn to him, snuggle into his chest where I'm always safe, but Griffin's attention snaps to us. A smile pulls at his lips, filled with the warmth I've grown to love. Love sticks in my throat, but even now, I can't deny it. This man standing in front of me is the same person I've spent the last few days with. The one I never wanted to let go of.

"I've got to go," he says into his phone and doesn't wait for the reply, dropping it onto the table, then stalks toward me.

My breath squeezes from my lungs with the force of his hug. He kisses my forehead. "How can I already miss you this much?"

I try to keep myself together, even though his words crash into me. I can't let myself hope for something more. I can't assume he feels the way that I do.

He doesn't let go of me when he asks Cole, "Why didn't you tell me you were coming home early?"

"What? Don't you like your surprise? Turnabout is fair play." His voice is closer, only inches behind me.

Griffin runs his hand up my back, circling his rough fingers around my neck, and swipes his thumb back and forth. The motion is so comforting I can't help but collapse into him.

"Best surprise I've ever received," he murmurs into my hair, refusing to let me slip even an inch. He's holding me so close, like he's afraid to let me go.

I ball the thick woven fabric of his sweater in my palms, afraid if I let him go, I'll wake up in the car, still driving away from him. I close my eyes, letting Griffin's forest scent consume me, and the world fades away. The only thing missing is Cole's heat pressing against my back.

As if summoned by my thoughts, a warm kiss is placed just above Griffin's hand on my neck. "As much as I hate to break you two up, we have a few things to discuss."

Griffin's chest inflates, and his arms tense around me before letting me go. He cups my jaw. "Remember this feeling, Baby Girl."

"There's no way I could forget." Uncertainty fills me, and I don't want to let him go, suddenly uneasy about what's going to happen next.

Griffin leads me to Cole, where he's sitting on the sofa, a glass of wine held out to me in his hand. I sit next to him, tucking my legs to my chest, and down it in one gulp.

He smirks. "There's no need for that. Just promise to hear us out."

Unease settles into me, and wishing I had another drink, I nod. There are a million things tumbling through my mind about what they're going to propose. Some kind of sharing situation where they pass me between them like I'm some sort of object? I know Cole loves me, but would he actually share me?

"We want you to move in with us," Griffin says matter-of-factly, like he didn't just flip the world upside down.

I'm hesitant to hope for what this can mean. "I can't just move in with you. Why would you even want that?"

Cole stiffens, and a muscle ticks in his jaw. The playful gleam is missing in his eyes as he says, "I've put a lot of thought into this, and it's the perfect solution.

You'll be closer to school. I can drive you back and forth. You won't have to live in your shitty apartment. No more forty-minute bus ride each way."

Everything he's saying makes sense, but I hate it. I hate that these are the reasons that he wants me to move in. That it's some rational thought process where the answers are simple but cold. I shake my head no when he pulls my hands into his and kisses my knuckles.

"Please, Eve. I'm not above begging. Please stay with us." His voice cracks around the vowels, none of the cool reasoning present.

My heart swells as he watches me. There's still a band wrapped around my chest, the one that says I could never be wanted. Never be anything more than a burden. I need to be honest about my feelings. There's no surviving this if there's any doubt remaining. I have to know if they want this for the same reasons I do.

I lean back, and Griffin's chest warms me. The rapid beating of his heart matching my own gives me the confidence to say, "It was hard for me when we left the cabin. When it was all over. I can't do that again. If I have you, I won't survive losing you."

Tears well as I wait for their response, desperately trying to build a wall before they reply, steadying myself for their answer.

Griffin wraps his hands around my middle, holding

me tight as Cole leans in and kisses me softly. "Listen to me, Eve. Hear my words clearly. We don't want to let you go. Ever. We want you to be a part of our family."

I turn to Griffin, needing to see his reaction. "It fucking killed me to leave you in that cabin. I'm pretty sure my entire office stayed away from me when I got there." He grips my chin. "There's nothing I want more than to come home to you *both* every night. Live with us. Be our family."

There's something I need to know. Something that will gnaw on me if I don't. "Do you love me?"

Griffin's laugh travels up my spine. "You have no idea how much I fucking love you. I think I fell the second I heard you speak."

This time, I can't stop my tears from welling over and traveling down my cheeks. "I love you. I...I love you both."

Cole's mouth is hot on my neck. "Good, it's settled. You'll move in."

"Are you sure you're okay with that?" I don't want to let either of them go, but I need to know how he feels.

"You kidding me? I couldn't be happier." He lifts me so my legs wrap around his waist and captures my mouth with his. "Promise us forever."

"I promise."

Chapter 17

Eve

GRIFFIN GROWLS from behind me and lifts me into the air. "That's all I need to hear."

He holds me against his chest as he walks us through a series of hallways to a bedroom, Cole holding on to my hand as he follows close behind. I don't have a chance to look around before I'm laid out on my back, the soft fabric rising around me as Griffin pushes me down into the mattress. I gasp as he presses down his rock-hard dick against my clit.

Cole leans down and kisses me senseless. I reach out to him, and my hand lands on muscle. At some point, he stripped out of his clothes, leaving him naked for me to see. My mouth waters as his abs flex, the cut V of his muscles leading down to where his cock stands tall between us. Precum pooling at the tip makes me want to lick it.

He groans and kneels on the bed. "You want this, Eve?"

I open my mouth wide and stick out my tongue in response.

"Fuck. You have no idea what you do to me," Cole says as he enters my mouth. He's so big it hurts, but all I want is to take in more of him.

"Look at how well you take his cock." My leggings slip down my legs, quickly followed by my underwear.

I moan, causing Cole's dick to grow even larger as Griffin descends between my thighs and licks a path up my core, sliding his fingers into me.

My hips move on their own while I swallow, trying to take Cole deeper, but no matter what I do, it's not enough. I need more. I need them to fill me until I can't think of anything but them.

Griffin's fingers are slick from my pussy as they travel down and press against my back hole. I nearly come off the bed at the unfamiliar sensation.

Cole retracts from my mouth as Griffin nips my thigh, holding me in place.

"I want to take you here." His breath fans over my clit, and my entire pussy clenches.

I've never tried this before, never wanted to, but something about it being him—*them*—has me nodding.

"Good girl," Griffin says.

Cole passes him a bottle, and cool liquid runs down the seam between my cheeks.

I tense.

"Relax, Baby Girl. We're going to make sure it feels good." He says it just as his finger breaches my rim.

Every one of my senses is focused on where he's touching me. The sensation is foreign, not quite uncomfortable, but not pleasurable either.

Cole's crisp green eyes take up my field of vision before he kisses me. His tongue is soft and gentle as it slides over mine, pulling my attention. Any unease slips away with his slow, teasing touch, and the new sensation of Griffin's finger turns sweet.

Cole doesn't release my mouth as he cups my breast, thumb rolling over my nipple just as Griffin stretches me wider, adding another finger.

I gasp, mouth falling open, each of his thrusts growing more intense. I squirm between them, unsure of how I'm feeling. Griffin licks my clit, ending any semblance of thought, and I feel nothing but good. The way he's filling is suddenly not enough. My clit pulses with each pass of his tongue, and my core clenches, a feeling of hollowness taking over.

I twist my fingers into Griffin's hair, forcing him down.

"I need more," I beg, not caring how I sound.

Cole removes my shirt, which is bunched around my shoulders, then lifts me onto his lap in the middle of the bed. My knees are on either side of him, and I cry out when his cock notches at my entrance, then fills me. I drop my head to his shoulder as he slowly rocks into me. With each of his movements, my clit rubs against his abs, sending shock waves down my spine.

"So good," I whisper into his neck, and his grip tightens on me, his movements growing faster.

"Don't make her come yet," Griffin says as he pours more liquid down the seam of my ass.

"Easier said than done," Cole grunts, stilling.

I bite down on Cole's shoulders as three fingers fill me. The dual sensations are almost too much as they both start moving. This time, I can't stop myself from rocking back, my hips moving on my own.

"That's my good girl," Griffin says, leaning over me and brushing my ear. He pulls his fingers out, and I whine at the loss of them.

His palm grips my ass, spreading my cheeks. "Do you want to take both of us?"

My head snaps up, eyes wide on a smiling Cole. "Can we do that?"

I can see him fight against his laugh, but he chokes it down. "Yeah, Eve. We can do that."

I glance back at Griffin. "Will it hurt?"

"I'll be careful."

Anticipation of having them both take me at once overcomes any fear I'm experiencing. "Okay."

Cole pulls me down so my chest is flat against his, and he spreads my legs wider with his knees. He brushes a strand of my hair back. "At any point, if you want to stop, we'll stop."

I take a deep breath. "I trust you."

With those words, Griffin presses his cock against my ass, circling the sensitive entrance before slowly breaching the rim.

My eyes roll back in my head, and Cole tucks it into the crook of his neck. "Bite me."

He doesn't jerk when I sink my teeth into him as Griffin gives me more. It doesn't hurt. I'm just so full that their cocks are pushing me past the point of sanity, into oblivion.

"I'm all the way in," Griffin grunts, his hands squeezing the blankets on either side of us. "You are so tight."

Cole's hands run up and down my side, over my hips and back. "Relax. You're doing such a great job taking us."

I hum, unable to respond, but my muscles ease more with each graze of his fingers.

"That's it."

I'm completely in their control, unable to move

myself when Griffin pulls back slowly, then pushes back in.

It's like electricity pierces through my head, sending shivers down my spine, and both men groan as I clench.

Cole stays still as Griffin penetrates me over and over. Even without moving, his heart pounds against mine, and his breath shudders out of him.

"Fuck, Griffin. I can feel you rub against me. It feels so fucking good."

His words unleash something in Griffin, and his thrusts turn ragged, harder and deeper each time. It's almost more than I can take.

Cole pulls me closer to him, kissing me wildly. His movements are as uncontrolled as Griffin's. I lean into the sensation of being filled in both holes, let it take over as I grind my clit into Cole and cry out their names.

My orgasm slams into me, turning my vision white as it crests over and over until I can't breathe, and my brain goes fuzzy.

Cole fills me with his cum as Griffin groans and coats my back with his before collapsing onto me, then pulling me to the side, pressing me between them.

They both kiss me all over until every inch of my skin feels worshiped.

"You're made for us." Cole runs his thumb along my bottom lip. "I love you so fucking much."

Griffin's head rests against the back of mine, and I can feel him nod. He gently kisses my neck.

"Thank you for being our family."

Chapter 18

Epilogue

A Few Months Later

Eve

Cole's still sleeping soundly when I slip out from under the covers, sliding one of his large gray T-shirts over my head. I can't even remember when I fell asleep. All I know is it started with Valentine's Day dinner and ended with all of us in bed. I've been beyond stressed with studying, and both men have been doing everything they can to take care of me. I swear it's like they think I'm a princess, and I haven't had to lift a finger in the months since I moved in with them. It's taken some time to get used to since it's the complete opposite of what I'm used to. Somehow, they make it feel natural, which has helped me immensely.

I pad my way into the kitchen, following the low,

gruff sound of Griffin's voice. At this point, I could recognize it in a crowd with my eyes closed. There's something in the way it makes me feel that's indescribable. I peek around the corner and freeze. I thought Griffin was on the phone, but his assistant is here, an iPad in his hand as he checks things off.

I'm about to flee into the privacy of our room when Griffin's attention turns to me, his lips quirking up into a warm smile.

"Morning, Baby Girl. Had a good sleep?"

I can feel my cheeks heating as I glance at Glenn, Griffin's long-term assistant, and back to the man I love. "Uh...yeah... I'm sorry to interrupt."

Griffin's brows pull low, and he gestures for me to come toward him. For a brief second, I think about what would happen if I defied him but disregard it when his eyes turn dark. I'll leave that for another time.

Entirely too aware of the fact I'm only wearing a shirt, I walk to Griffin, grateful that the island is between us and Glenn. At least my important bits are covered. I'm still tugging my shirt down when he slides his coffee toward me.

"It's okay. I can just make my own."

"Why would you do that? This one's hot and ready." Griffin's arms bracket me, his warm chest pressing against my back.

It hasn't been long since I noticed Griffin's changed how he makes his coffee to be the same as me, and it's not the first time he's given me his. At this point, it seems like that's been his intention all along. Lost in our own little world, I almost miss Glenn saying good morning.

"M...morning." I give him a shy smile, still uncomfortable to be out here with him while I'm dressed this way. I've noticed Griffin likes to push my limits with an audience. I'll have to ask him if it's a kink or something.

Soft lips press against the top of my head.

"Continue." Griffin's chest reverberates over my back as he speaks to his assistant, distracting me more with each word.

Glenn ticks off items one by one. "You have a meeting at ten with the CEO of MRS Tech. An eleven o'clock with the manager of logistics. You have a half-hour break for lunch. I'll need you to review and sign some documents during that time. At twelve, you have a meeting with..."

His voice fades out as rough fingers trail up the back of my thighs, sending a shiver in their wake. Heat floods me as Griffin's hand moves until he's teasing the edge of my panties before dipping under and gripping my ass. He kneads the muscle, all the while speaking calmly to his assistant like he's not driving me absolutely crazy.

I gasp when his hand cups my bare core, sliding through where I'm wet.

I try to cover it with a cough. "Sorry, coffee went down the wrong pipe."

Griffin's chuckle fans over my neck, causing my already heated body to ignite. I need him to stop what he's doing to me before I start begging for more.

My hips rock back against my will, and he groans before saying, "Clear my day."

"I'm sorry, sir?" Glenn replies in disbelief.

"I won't be going in today." Griffin punctuates the sentence, thrusting his fingers in deep. "I have other plans."

"But—"

My underwear is being pushed down my thighs.

"That's all. I'll see you tomorrow." Griffin's tone leaves no room for discussion.

"Ah...okay, sir. I'll take care of it." It's clear he thinks it's an impossible task, but he doesn't argue. He averts his eyes and says on his way out, "Ms. Eve. Have a good day."

The second he's out the door, Griffin drops to his knees behind me, pressing his palm into my back until my stomach touches the cool marble. His tongue runs up my seam as he tastes me.

146

He hums. "You're already so wet for me."

I'm rocking back into him when he stands, sitting me on the counter and removing my shirt. He slides his thumb over his bottom lip.

"How the fuck did we get so lucky?" he says before capturing my nipple in his mouth, causing me to arch further into his touch.

"Can I join?" Cole asks from behind us.

Griffin pulls back. "Already got her ready for you."

"Good, I'm hungry," Cole replies and lifts me off the counter, pulling a giggle from me as he heads toward our room.

We've had sex on every surface in this house, meaning whatever they have planned is more than the usual. A shiver runs through me in anticipation.

Cole sets me on the bed and doesn't look away as he removes his clothes. He crawls over me, then flips us so he's laid out with his back to the bed, and I'm facing him, my knees on either side of him. I can't help myself from rubbing my clit against his hard cock, causing all of us to groan.

"That's it. Make yourself feel good." Cole's hands grip my ass as he guides my hips back and forth, coating his length with my wetness.

I suck in a breath when he fills me completely. No matter how many times I take him, it still takes me a second to adjust to his width.

My fingers dig into his shoulders as he moves, filling me over and over.

Firm hands spread my ass apart. "Fuck. You should see yourself right now, Baby Girl."

Griffin's words urge me on, and I thrust my hips backward, matching Cole's rhythm.

Warm liquid pools between my cheeks as Griffin rubs it in. I expect him to slide a finger into my back hole, but I suck in a breath when he presses against where Cole's already filling me.

I squirm against his touch, not sure I can handle what happens next.

Cole lifts my chin so I look at him. "We'll take care of you."

Tension flows out of me, and I collapse to his chest, surrendering to them. They've never given me a reason not to trust them.

"That's it," Griffin says, his finger circling my core. "Take a deep breath."

I inhale.

"Let it out."

He breaches the rim as I exhale, and my eyes roll back. It's not exactly painful, but I can't describe it as good either.

It's not until Cole moves again that any discomfort turns to pleasure.

"That's it. Breathe for us," Griffin says as he

presses another finger into me.

I moan so loud I'm positive the neighbors hear me. My body's shaking as it stretches to adjust.

Cole pushes a strand of hair behind my ear. "That's my girl. You're doing so good."

My core pulses as my orgasm grows deep in my stomach, each of their thrusts driving me higher until I'm crying out with my release.

I'm exhausted and collapse onto Cole, his pounding heart the only thing I can hear.

Warm hands rub my back as I slowly come to my senses.

I finally have the strength to lift up. "You didn't come?"

"We are nowhere near done," Griffin says from beside me.

He's kneeling on the bed, his ass to his ankles, making a shelf with his thighs.

He reaches out a hand, helping stabilize me. "Sit on my lap, Baby Girl."

I crawl over to him, and he grips my hips, twisting so I'm facing away from him, and immediately fills me with his cock. "You feel so good."

I let him take my weight as he lowers us so we're leaned back on an angle. The position leaves me on display for Cole, who's looking at me with darkened eyes.

His tongue slides over his teeth like he's hungry and I'm breakfast. He kisses me soundly, stealing my breath.

"Make her come. We need her nice and soft."

Cole groans before descending, his mouth pressed against my clit. "My pleasure."

The feeling of Griffin's cock filling me again and again while Cole sucks my clit is more than I can take. I shatter around them instantly.

My head's dropped back, resting on Griffin's shoulder, too exhausted to hold it up.

"I want you to watch," Griffin says as he reaches down, grasping Cole's cock and coating it in lube before guiding it to my already full core.

I stiffen, a trace of fear traveling down my spine.

"It's okay. We've got you." Cole drops his forehead against mine. "Do you want to keep going?"

Swallowing hard, I nod.

"Good. Now, relax."

"That's easier said than done," I joke, but it's cut off as Cole enters me inch by inch.

The sensation is mind-bending. I didn't know it was possible to take them both, let alone that it would feel this good.

My lungs burn from holding my breath until my head tingles and black spots fill my vision.

Griffin's large hand cups my breast. "Breathe, baby. You've got this. Look how well you're taking us."

There's no semblance of thought. I'm lost to them, following whatever they say as they both alternate their thrusts, pushing into me repeatedly.

Cole presses kisses into my neck. "That's my girl. I can feel your pussy pulse around us."

A wave of pleasure crests and then crashes over me again until an overwhelming pressure forms below my navel.

"Wait," I cry out, but they just push into me harder, both of them chasing their own climax.

They groan in unison, their hot cum shooting into me.

My body trembles as my muscles tighten, trying to hold this unfamiliar feeling back. I'm lost to it when they pull out, causing my orgasm to seize my whole body, drenching them in my release.

I come over and over again, until the bed's soaked around us.

It's several moments later before I'm coherent enough for embarrassment to crawl up my neck.

"I'm sorry. That's never happened before."

Cole meets my gaze. "What are you sorry about? That was fucking hot."

Griffin kisses my temple. "You're perfect."

They wash me, my body too liquid to hold myself up, wrap me in a towel, and sit me on the floor in front of the sofa. I rest between Griffin's firm legs, breathing in his forest scent as I attempt to watch the movie playing on the TV. Long fingers stroke through my hair before a comb untangles the ends.

I reach up. "I can do that."

"You're exhausted. Just relax."

I don't have the strength to argue with him, so I drop my head forward as he carefully combs out the tangles until my wet hair falls smoothly around me. I already feel cherished when Cole brings me a glass of Gatorade, telling me to make sure I finish it.

If they weren't trying so hard, it would be ridiculous. Instead, warmth fills my chest with everything they do.

The buzz of a blow dryer turning on pulls my attention, but Griffin guides my head to the front as he dries my hair.

"You don't have to do that. It can dry on its own," I mumble, aware it's almost impossible to hear me.

Griffin's rough fingers squeeze the back of my neck. "Enough of that. I don't want you getting sick."

If he wants to, I'm not going to stop him. My eyes

close, the heat relaxing me further until I'm seconds from passing out.

Griffin lifts me over his knees when my hair's dry. "Don't fall asleep yet."

Cole kneels in front of us, his lip caught between his teeth. He looks nervous, and I want to soothe it away. There's nothing they can say to me I wouldn't like.

Griffin and Cole have some kind of silent conversation, and Cole nods.

"Eve, we love you."

I squeeze Griffin's arm so he knows he's included. "I love you too."

"You have brought a light into our lives that I never thought could be possible," Griffin says as he guides me so I can see both of them.

Cole pulls a small jewelry box from behind him that he's been hiding. "I know it hasn't been long, but I'm positive meeting you was fate. You've completed our family like no one else could."

Tears sting my eyes at his sincerity.

"Baby Girl, if you'll have us, we want to spend the rest of our lives with you. Be a family. Forever."

I'm already nodding before he finishes speaking.

Cole takes my hand gently and slides a simple gold band around my finger. "Legally, we can't all be married, but we'll know. This ring symbolizes my love for you. That it'll never waver."

My eyes are glued to the golden glint of the metal.

Griffin clears his throat, holding out his own band. "If you'll have me, wear this so everyone knows you're taken."

"Yes." He guides the ring over my knuckle, fitting perfectly against Cole's.

I swallow hard. "I just wish I had something to give you."

"I hope you don't mind. I took the liberty of purchasing matching rings for me and Griffin."

I smile at him. He's always one step ahead of me. I take the rings from him and slide one on each of their ring fingers while professing my love for each of them.

Tears pool before overflowing my lashes, running down my cheeks.

"Thank you. Thank you for loving me. Thank you for saving me. Thank you for giving me the family I never knew I could have."

Both men lean in and kiss me and say together as if they practiced, "Always and forever."

RULES OF OUR OWN

NEED ANOTHER SPICY THROUPLE?
Read this **MMF Hockey Romance**

Blurb:

Somehow, I've landed myself a do-over and this time we aren't screwing it up. This time, I don't want her all to myself. This time we're going to share.

Mia:

The second the Boston Bruins star forward steps out of the villa bathroom, looking like a god in nothing but a low slung towel...I should turn around and beg for a different room.

When his tall, dark and broody teammate walks in offering to share the villa...I should run.

And when they offer me one weekend of no strings attached fun...I should absolutely say no.

But I've never been good at doing what I'm supposed to.

Alex:

Three nights wasn't enough. Not when I still wake up dreaming about her. About them.

Imagine our surprise when our new neighbor ends up being the girl we've both been obsessing over.

This time, we won't lose her.

This time, things will be different.

This time...we're ready to share.

River:

They're mine to own, possess, consume. They just don't know it yet.

Rules Of Our Own is an interconnected stand-alone NHL Hockey Romance with a MMF why-choose style HEA.

Forced proximity, bi-awakening, where the guys are obsessed with her as they are with each other.

Want more?

READ HERE

Thank you!

I want to give the biggest thank you ever to everyone who made this book possible.

Aly, who keeps me motivated.

Jen, who keeps me positive.

Nicole, who makes sure I actually have the characters take their clothes off and there's no extra arms in sex scenes.

My readers, who make this all possible.

Xoxoxoxo

Made in the USA
Monee, IL
04 December 2024

72245732R00095